Adrift on the Salish Sea

from Point No Point to Deception Pass

A novel of Whidbey Island

The story that follows is a work of fiction set in a real time and place and community with occasional flights of fantasy and minor distortions of time. All of the characters are fictional, and any resemblance to real people is by chance.

Adrift on the Salish Sea from Point No Point to Deception Pass
Copyright 2015 Mladen Serafimov. All rights reserved.

No part of this book may be used or reproduced in any manner without written permission except in the case of brief quotations.

Nettle Hollow, Langley, WA, 98260 USA, 2015

"Let us try then what Love will do: for if men did once see we love them, we soon should find they would not harm us. Force may subdue, but Love gains: and he that forgives first, wins the laurel."

William Penn

Prologue

Today I turned 70. It is not so very old, but all the same, I know I am no longer young. My joints hurt at night after some sorry excuse for an honest day's work. And I mourn the passage of so many loved ones, family and friends. So many, it seems. Yes, and I am growing wearier of it all, but not so weary that I no longer care what happens around me. So long as I draw a breath and have enough sense to know the difference between right and wrong, I will make my preference known.

You see, I learned a long time ago about the cost of ignorance and thoughtlessness. Let me tell you a little about it.

Chapter One

Take a breath, let it in, let it out, you're still alive, man, for another day. Most of the fools out there have no idea what a daily miracle that actually is. Not me. But that doesn't mean that I know the first thing about living, really living. I've already learned too much about death and dying, I guess.

These thoughts passed through Skeeter's mind as he laid the hot chainsaw down on the soft, damp, green carpet of moss on the forest floor and rolled his third cigarette of the day between swigs from a chilly can of Rainier beer. His back ached and there was a burning pain in his right shoulder. He felt like an old man at 23. But then, he had been through "some weird shit," as he sometimes told people.

He pulled a book of paper matches from his timber cruiser's vest and struggled to light one in the stiff breeze coming off Point No Point on the shore below. Then he rested with a smoke, perched on a fresh stump that offered an unobstructed view of the choppy water between Whidbey Island and the mainland, five miles away, somewhat obscured by a fine veil of mist.

To the south he could see the ferry boat, the Kulshan, slowly making its way from Mukilteo on the mainland side to the Clinton Ferry dock on the island, with a load of some fifteen cars just barely distinguishable on its open deck. The crossing took about 25 minutes on a good day and closer to an hour during a storm. He smiled as he remembered the day, years ago, when his dad was running late for the ferry, and he beeped his horn at the top of the hill as he saw the ferry pulling out, and the captain reversed the engine and pulled back in in order to hold the ferry for him.

You could do that back in an earlier day, but you wouldn't want to try it today, in 1977. Times were changing and people weren't so easy going any more. Maybe it was economic pressures with the downturn, or the fact that more people on the island meant more need to maintain public order. On the other hand, just last week, when he had an errand to the mainland, an old school chum who was piloting the ferry that day, let him join him on the bridge and even let him steer the boat for a while, just for the fun of it. He smiled as he recalled veering the ferry far to one side and then veering it back the other way, just to see how it handled. Passengers must have thought the pilot was avoiding debris in the water or some such thing.

It had been a mild winter with only an occasional wet snow that melted after a day. Now, with the approach of the spring equinox the weather remained unsettled. Billowing, dark cumulus clouds coming in from the storm bound convergence zone between the mountains and the water to the east dumped hail one minute and then the next minute the sun would poke through the clouds. To the west he could see larger patches of blue sky looking ever so inviting over the rain shadow, a region where rainfall was a fraction of what it was to the north or south. It was a patch of territory that stretched from the Olympic Mountain coastline of the Peninsula extending on over from Port Townsend to Coupeville on central Whidbey Island. Strange country this, with its jumble of microclimates.

Again this year there was the promise of spring and of new and renewed life in the air. This should have had an invigorating effect on a young man, but Skeeter mainly found himself just staring rather listlessly into space. He had some vague awareness of how the forest enfolded him in its emerald green as he perched on this hillside 200 feet above and a quarter mile back from the island coastline. A chill breeze made his ears tingle, despite the steamy heat rising from his shirt collar after an hour of chainsaw work. There was a pleasant scent of wet humus and fungi in the air, and the dappled mix of varying shades of green of the foliage was pleasing to his eyes. He found some temporary peace in these moments out in the woods, away from people. Though there was no real escape from the chronic lethargy and depression that had held him in its unsparing grip for nigh on two years now.

No coincidence that that time matched the time since his discharge from the army. He hadn't been in combat more than half a day when the truck he was riding in took a mortar round that left him riddled with shrapnel, some of which plagued him to the present day. Half a day in combat. What a joke. The new, raw recruit that no one in the platoon had wanted to talk to, since no one knew how long he might actually be with them. And weren't they psychic, it seemed, since the medics ended up hauling his sorry ass off the battlefield before he could even fully unpack his duffel in one of the tents. Then, it was months of surgeries and hospital stays followed by more months recovering in a bed in his old room at the family farm.

Fuck it all, he thought to himself. That seemed to be his internal mantra, to be repeated in his head after only brief intervals, throughout the day. Did it help him get through another day? Perhaps, though if he were honest, he would have to give more credit to the little black mutt terrier who sat in the forest duff a short distance away, his constant companion, who shared his present hermit's life in a one room shack out in the woods near South Whidbey State Park.

He had been kind of pissed off when his dad had set the puppy on his bed one day last year and told him that he needed a pal. Moping around the house was about all he did back then, and he didn't want some little mutt to take care of. But he had to admit that he was fond of the little fucker now, even if he did just call him Rat Dog. With time there was a touch of affection to it, whenever he said that name.

....

The town of Langley was relatively deserted, so there was plenty of parking in front of the old, weathered clapboard buildings on First Street, fronting the water. The little downtown had a slightly seedy look to it. In fact, all of the towns along Puget Sound had taken on a similar look of benign neglect, ever since the Boeing Corporation's fortunes had declined in the early 70's, leading to large-scale lay-offs at their plants there. Since it was pretty much a one company town, many former workers had left in search of better work prospects elsewhere, prompting the local sick joke: "Would the last person leaving Seattle, please turn out the lights?"

It was late afternoon when Skeeter parked and entered the Doghouse Tavern. The two story, boxy old building appeared dingy and dark as he stepped inside. But the stained, ancient wallpaper and dusty corners didn't look all that bad in the dim light, while the long, narrow, polished maple wood bar drew the eye.

The Doghouse had a reputation as a friendly, inviting village tavern. Families with kids even came in the side door and sat at the tables in the back room. Sure, there had been a shooting out on the street in front not long ago, some outsiders choosing to settle a score on someone else's turf. But that was just a bizarre episode. Even the drunken spat was rare. The sixty plus year old bar welcomed all who behaved themselves and it had become a meeting place for diverse groups of locals as well as newcomers and passing tourists in the summertime.

At the moment there were about two dozen patrons in the tavern. They all perked their ears up as a glass crashed to the floor and shattered into small pieces, followed by a mumbled curse. But no one wanted to give it any further visible attention.

The five "hippies" sitting at the front window table near the door, who were only slightly noticeable for their long hair, colorful second hand clothes and known preference for weed over alcohol, barely noticed the shattering glass. There was some trouble brewing in the local woods over a planned clear cut that had the "tree huggers" upset, and they were having a heated argument among themselves.

The few local boys at the bar just kind of rolled their eyes at each other, as if to say, somebody must be drunk again. They were noticeable as a group for still being dressed in their work clothes, Levi's, flannel shirts and vibram-soled leather boots. They leaned toward cheap beer after a day's work out in the woods or in the farm fields or out on the water, although they weren't against smoking some weed when the opportunity arose. Two local guys who sat with their dolled up girl friends at a table opposite the bar, laughing and talking a bit loudly as they tried to impress their dates, grew quiet at the sound of the glass. An older couple, newly retired professional people, recently resettled in an island beach house, sitting at a table next to them, momentarily looked up, then continued talking quietly to each other.

There was only one guy that seemed totally oblivious to outside events. Skeeter had met him before in the tavern. A quiet, young guy, obviously from off island, who sat at the end of the bar and nursed a beer, surrounded by beat up old notebooks and stray sheets of paper.

"What you up to, man?" Skeeter asked him. The young man looked up, only then noticing Skeeter standing there. He had obviously been totally absorbed in the papers in front of him.

"Writing a book on the history of the island, an environmental and social history of the interactions of land and people," he mumbled, slightly annoyed by the intrusion.

"Why would you want to write about a fucked up place like this? I've been here all my life, except for a little trip to 'Nam, and I don't see a whole lot around here worth writing about."

At this, the young man stared hard at Skeeter, frowned and then, after a brief pause, said: "Maybe it's a more interesting place than you imagine."

To which Skeeter replied. "Maybe it's a more fucked up place than you imagine."

He asked Skeeter, "What does your family do for a living?"

The question seemed innocent enough, but there was something off putting about it, like they were some sort of interesting specimen of indigenous fauna. Skeeter just frowned and picked up his beer and headed toward the back of the tavern.

As he passed by the hippies he couldn't help glancing their way. Kind of interesting to him for their free spirited ways, but an opinionated bunch. Their strong opinions about a lot of things, some of them local things that they really knew very little about, could kind of piss him off at times.

Then he passed by the table with the retired folks. Now there was someone to appreciate for their contribution to the local economy. He'd been hired a few times to help restore some old shore cottage into a full time home. But he frowned as he thought about how such people could buy an old farm or beach house from elderly folks who couldn't afford to just pass it on to their own cash strapped children, most of whom were just getting started in their own family lives. Since a lot of these people were coming up from California, there was more than one car on the island with a bumper sticker that read: "Don't Californicate Washington state!"

In addition to a pint of Rainier beer on tap, Skeeter had ordered some smoked salmon on sourdough bread from the frowning, middle aged, baseball cap wearing owner bar tender, which he took to a table in the back room with a fine view of Saratoga Passage out the east windows. The clouds had rolled in and the water between Camano and Whidbey Islands had turned a steely gray. The green of the heavily forested high bank shoreline of Camano, some two or three miles away, appeared muted and with a touch of gloom in the fading light.

Suddenly Skeeter gaped in wonder as a great dark form emerged from the water about a hundred yards off shore. Was it a great gray whale that had momentarily surfaced? If it was, it would be plunging back down into the shallow depths to take another long scoop of shrimp rich sea sand into its enormous mouth, to be strained of its nutritious bounty before being once again returned to the sea bottom. The grays came up the coast every year to feed in the Sound for a few months. They had been doing this for as long as anyone could remember. But wasn't March a bit early for them?

Only the resident orcas, or Killer Whales, among the whales, spent more time in Puget Sound. Skeeter still had trouble sleeping sometimes when he was reminded of the terrible scene he had witnessed the year before, when a crew had herded the local orcas into the end of Penn Cove and then netted some of the babies for subsequent sale to aquariums for water shows like those at Sea World in Florida. The thrashing and the pitiful cries of separated mothers and babies would haunt him for the rest of his life. It was rumored that some of the young whales had not survived the attempt at capture and lay at the bottom of the Sound, in netting weighted down by rocks to hide the evidence. So he'd heard, and he wouldn't be surprised if it were true. Sometimes humanity really sucked, he thought to himself.

And speaking of humanity that really sucked, here came a big, beefy guy that he'd known all his life, who usually drank over at the VFW Hall. He came in and sat down at the next table after giving Skeeter a brief nod of recognition. That guy never had liked him, and that cool streak had gotten colder after Skeeter had shown up at the Hall a while back wearing his t-shirt that read: " Southeast Asian War Games, 1965-75 Second Place." He had thought the shirt just plain fucking hilarious, but that didn't seem to be the consensus. 'Screw 'em,' he thought to himself.

He looked back out the window and there was the whale, breaking the surface again, some 200 yards off shore. The whale was easily 40 feet in length, but what the heck was it? Must be a gray. It almost looked like one of the rock formations that rose and then fell back into the depths with the tide at the north end of the island at Deception Pass. It glided silently and seemingly effortlessly through the darkening water, its sleek hide glistening in the remaining light. A creature that was utterly at home in the cold, uninviting waters of Puget Sound. A man had all of fifteen minutes in that same water before hypothermia incapacitated him and death soon followed.

Where were men at home? He wondered to himself. No one he knew ever seemed to be content. Human beings seemed to always be restlessly stirring. Not one seemed to be able to really sit still and relax. If they weren't busy messing with other creatures, they were jerking each other around. Fighting over turf or pride or just for the hell of it. And like his neighbor at the next table, usually making a pig of themselves. There he was, shoveling food in his mouth while swilling a full pitcher of beer by himself, and chain smoking the whole time. And, no doubt, when he got bored with all of that he would remember how much he despised his fellow man, in this case, Skeeter, and start needling him with petty insults.

"Hey, you been out fishing at all this winter?" He chose that moment to call out to Skeeter. "Fuck of a lot of fish out there, man. Pacific cod, some decent rockfish... Or is that piece of shit you call a boat, too leaky to get you out on the water?"

Skeeter wanted to totally ignore the nasty prick. But a nasty guy like this one didn't easily take no for an answer. He had been a bully all his life. Skeeter had unpleasant memories of him going all the way back to grade school. Skeeter's dad had suggested that the family had a long, proud tradition of bullying, and when Skeeter, as a kid, had admitted to getting picked on by this most recent generation's representative of the ancient art, his dad had tried to advise him with a little story from his own youth. "I remember one day," his dad had said, "when Jack (the present Jack's father) was chasing me around as usual, to beat me up, when I thought to myself, what's the point of running, he always catches me, and he always beats me up. So I stopped, all of the sudden, and smashed Jack in the mouth with my fist, and he ran off crying."

Nice story, and nice if it were always so easy to deal with pricks like this guy. Best to just humor him a bit and slip away at the first opportunity. "Yeah, my boat really sucks. Maybe I'll turn it into kindling to keep me warm through the winter and buy something to replace it."

"You pathetic little shit, do you expect me to believe that you could afford to buy anything but another shipwreck?"

Skeeter finished his beer and muttered something about "having to see a man about a dog..."and headed for the door. But Jack stood up and began to follow him out.

As they approached the door, they passed the table of "tree huggers." There was a red haired girl among them who caught his attention, and as she saw Skeeter looking at her she made momentary eye contact, and then ducked her head to act as if it hadn't happened. Skeeter just gave a slight nod and kept on going. Jack, however much he might have wanted to continue riding Skeeter, couldn't resist a chance to give "the hippies" some trouble.

"If any of you so much as touch any of my buddies' logging equipment, we'll make you real sorry you ever set foot on this friendly island," Jack bellowed as he passed by their table. Skeeter just stared ahead and quickened his pace, eager to distance himself from the drunken pig, while knowing full well that the group of them were likely to assume that he and Jack were together. The bartender glared at Jack, a warning to him not to mess with his customers.

Skeeter suddenly remembered that his aging parents had asked him to stop by to help out with a few chores on the old homestead today. Although the light was fading, he could probably still help his dad get some firewood moved before it was too dark to see, if he hurried. So he quietly slipped out the swinging saloon style double doors into the fading light. He could see out of the corner of his eye that Jack had decided to follow him out. He must have lost interest in whatever further trouble he could provoke in the bar.

Skeeter was about to hop into his truck when he saw Jack coming his way out of the growing darkness. He stepped back from the truck, just watching as the big, wobbly drunk approached. 'Had he really been running from nasty bullies like Jack since grade school?' "Oh, shit," he muttered.

As Jack arrived at his side, his alcohol dulled mind was still working overtime to come up with the next insult to hurl at Skeeter . "Hey, you runt, I ain't through with you yet." And he grabbed Skeeter by the shoulder.

Skeeter tensed. 'What the fuck?' He wished that he had made it into the truck, where he had a shotgun hidden behind the seat. Was he going to have to endure more nasty taunts before he could finally extricate himself and head for home. 'What is it about me that seems to provoke this guy?' He asked himself.

"Why, what is there left to say?" asked Skeeter, his voice a little thin and weak. It reminded him of times past, as a kid, when Jack had bullied him, eventually getting him to cry after showing him who was the bigger and tougher of the two of them.

"Not really much to say," Jack stumbled a bit, his speech so slurred that Skeeter had to strain to hear what he was saying. "You just need to know that I don't like you. I don't like the way you slink around town with your whiny little bitch tone of voice. And I don't like the way you look down on this great country. Running it down. You're asking to have your face pushed in. You know that? I would do it right now, but I would rather keep you guessing about when you're gonna get what you've been asking for, for a while now. You got that?" Jack's face held a malevolent little grin, as he continued to hold Skeeter by the shoulder.

Skeeter didn't know what to say or do. Jack let go of him then and stepped back. That gave Skeeter a chance to hop into the truck and start the engine. The muffler immediately started to growl angrily, which reminded him that he had better open the window so that the exhaust fumes coming up through the floor didn't kill him and the dog during the drive. As he pulled away, with Jack standing there at the curb and just watching him, he felt a shudder run through him and the blood rush to his face.

Maybe he really was the worthless worm that Jack had him pegged for. He didn't really like himself all that much, and he hated Jack, and he didn't feel much of anything for most of the people around him. What good was he to himself or anyone else really? He thought to himself as he drove.

A light snow was falling now, and he kind of wished that the rubber on the wipers wasn't quite so rotted, so that he could see a little better through the windshield. He tried to concentrate on the drive out of town, squinting through the blurry windshield to try and see anything he should avoid in his path. The little town was already shutting down for the winter evening as he drove off. He enjoyed the fact that you parked your car and got out and walked around town and met your fellow humans eye to eye here, rather than do the town through drive around shopping, as you did in the sprawl of the business districts of other towns. Maybe it could get too personal though, as the current situation with bully Jack suggested.

He cruised on past The Clyde Theatre and the Moonraker Bookstore and past the entrance to the marina and on up past the old high school and the red barns of the county fairground. But instead of turning left, as he'd originally planned, he decided that he was too drunk to go by his folk's place. He would follow Langley and then Maxwelton Road on out to the highway instead, and then head north toward home.

The snowflakes illuminated in his headlights sparkled like a million stars rushing by as his starship plunged through some far off galaxy. The low rumble of the engine and the constant flow of the flakes were mesmerizing. Fortunately, the seat belt buckle under his butt kept digging into his tailbone, the pain helping keep him awake on the ride home. Funny how almost every car nowadays had seat belts, but he had yet to see anyone among the people he knew actually bother to use one.
Chapter Two

It was a Stellar Jay, that had found a way into the shed and was squawking over his venison, that pulled him out of his sleep the next morning. He and the dog hadn't budged from the old armchair all night. Would have been nice to get his clothes off, but he'd been too far gone for that. A few coals remained from last night's fire, making it fairly easy to stoke up a blaze once again. An opaque gray roof lay over the dark hemlock, spruce and fir forest. It could have seemed gloomy, but he knew that a hand rolled bit of tobacco, a little Maxwell House coffee boiled on top of the stove, and a bowl of dry dog food to shut Rat Dog up, and he would feel almost ready for the world. Until he noticed the shotgun cradled in his lap and he remembered the nightmare, and the usual paranoia that overwhelmed him at night. "Oh fuck," he muttered to himself. And Rat Dog gave a little squeaky whine as if he commiserated with his alpha's plight.

He might have stayed there all morning just watching the flock of little gray Dark-eyed juncoes with their black hooded heads flutter around and peck at the hunk of suet he had hung up on a branch near the window. Unfortunately, the meat out on the rack out back wouldn't wait. A day or two of hanging wasn't a bad idea, but some of these newcomers to the island, especially the hippie tree huggers, couldn't be trusted not to turn him in to the local cops for poaching, if they came upon his venison. Why didn't he get a big, nasty pit bull or something, instead of this little Rat Dog, to keep snoopers away?

But he needed to eat something first, and there was nothing worth mentioning, on that score, in the cabin. So he put on his wool jacket and the hat with the ear flaps, locked an unhappy Rat Dog in the cabin and considered how he might get to the Greenbank Store without having to use what little gas he had left in his truck. He set off on a path through the forest that eventually led to an access to Bakken Road. Then he hiked the last quarter mile down Bakken and ducked into the field next to the progressive hall and entered the Greenbank Store through the rear entrance.

The old barn red building had been there for nearly a hundred years, part of a complex built back at the turn of the century by Calvin Phillips, founder of the Greenbank Farm, down the hill, with its 140 acres of loganberries. Pommerelle's loganberry wine was the fine product of the farm. Skeeter had often sampled his share of the wine on cold, dark winter nights after helping bring in the harvest during the summer.

He glanced around to make sure he hadn't been followed and then climbed the indoor stairs to the little loft restaurant, and ordered a bowl of bean soup "made by the navy," according to the sign made by the ex-sailor who ran the place. It hit the spot, but not the gloomy, suspicious stares of the proprietor. Something really bad had happened in their family and every young male on the loose somehow came under suspicion. It really sucked, for them and those around them. The restaurant owner's daughter, only recently married, had been found out back of her home. According to police reports some person or persons, unknown, had smothered her to death. Her family was devastated and every young man for miles around, including her own devastated husband, was a potential suspect. The island seemed like a peaceful, sleepy backwater, but like elsewhere, there was always an undercurrent of violence that occasionally took someone under. And most recently it was an innocent, young, pretty girl who had waitressed until recently right there in the restaurant where he now slurped his bowl of soup. Why should he feel so special about having violent death potentially breathing down his neck today?

He found an old guy at the store with a pickup truck and too much time on his hands, who gave him a lift back to the trail head into his place. When he arrived back at the cabin, he finished processing the deer meat and loaded it into the truck. Then he and Rat Dog set off for Sebering's, at Bayview, where he would rent a freezer locker.

This morning Skeeter drove with particular care. And he couldn't help darting his eyes left and right and glancing in the rearview mirror every so often, searching out danger. The old shotgun was wedged under the front seat. Maybe he would be able to reach it when the time came that he needed it.

He pulled out of the forest onto Day Road and a few minutes later he rounded the turn onto Lagoon Point Road. As he passed the little old shack where crusty old bachelor, Charlie Christin lived, he gave the horn a little toot. He had worked on a few construction jobs with the old coot and his small bulldozer. Charlie, who had lived here since the 1920's, slept with a box of dynamite for blasting stumps safely tucked under his bed. Every second word out of the old guy was "cocksucking," "sonofabitch," or some such curse word, followed by a spit to the ground. Maybe his lifelong bachelorhood was more than self-imposed, thought Skeeter as he glanced over at Charlie's little shack.

As he rounded the corner onto Smugglers Cove Road and turned left in front of the Lagoon Point Firehouse, he was reminded of how he had had to put up with some bad jokes at the local fire station suggesting that Skeeter might be Charlie's long lost, illegitimate son. Was he really that much like the old curmudgeon?

The crowd at the Lagoon Point firehouse had been a bit cool toward him ever since he had gotten in an argument with them over whether or not the ground water on Whidbey actually flowed under Puget Sound from the Olympic Peninsula, making the supply almost limitless, or whether it came from limited underground pools of what fell from the skies. Skeeter was of the opinion that it was local and limited to forested watersheds. The others believed the claim of local well drillers and developers that there was an unlimited supply coming from deep springs from the Peninsula. Skeeter's last word on the subject, that had pissed off the local crew, was: "My point is that if I pee in that ravine near my cabin, the water that you drink gets a little saltier down here at Lagoon Point."

As he passed the turn into Lagoon Point, off Smugglers Cove Road, he noted that the street sign and the big white sign welcoming motorists to the Lagoon Point Community were now back in proper order. A while back in a fit of outrage, after the good homeowners down on the beach community had chased Skeeter off their beach during the fall silver salmon run, he had altered their signs with a little paint, erasing the La in Lagoon.

As they made their way south on Smugglers Cove Road, the sun emerged from the clouds and the steel gray waters of Admiralty Inlet to the west suddenly turned emerald blue, and the snow on the Olympic Mountains beyond the water over on the peninsula gleamed like a set of freshly cleaned teeth. As they drove by South Whidbey State Park on Smugglers Cove Road they could see a crowd gathered around some loggers and their equipment on the east side of the road. Long-haired youths and a sprinkling of older folks with grey hair stood or sat in front of the machinery, the skidders, trucks and gear, blocking or interfering with the men's work. "Fucking hippies," he muttered to himself. Then he saw a guy he knew on the crew, somebody he'd met in a bar over in Darrington a while back. So he pulled over onto the shoulder and hopped out and went over to the presently idled workman.

"Hey, Guy, how's it going?" he said to the logger, who was busy at the moment cleaning his chainsaw and trying to ignore the protesters gathered around their equipment.

"Hey, that you, Skeeter Jensen? Been a while. How you doin'? Looks like it ain't going at the moment, until the police come and clear this bunch out. So how you been?"

"Can't complain. Any chance of some work with your crew, or maybe just some firewood from the site?"

"Not much chance of work, but maybe some wood for you from the slash later."

Then a woman dressed in a flannel shirt, blue jeans and a green nylon down-filled vest peeled herself off from the crowd of protesters and approached them. Skeeter remembered her now from the bar the night before. She was slightly lean and agile in her movements. She projected a certain confident strength as she strode up to where they stood talking. Her shaggy red hair and intense, blazing green eyes were such a distraction that both men stopped talking and focused all of their attention on her. "You guys approve of what you're doing here? This 200 acres is the last stand of old growth forest on the island. Why not leave it, get your lumber from somewhere else?"

"Didn't you just hear that park ranger say that these old trees are full of bugs? That it'd be good to clean 'em out and plant some healthy young stuff in their place," said the young logger.

"So there are insects in the bark of these big old trees, what do you think the woodpeckers are doing, they are eating them, and making some cavities in the bark that birds, bats and squirrels will make homes in. It's called forest ecology. Everything here is connected, dependent..." She argued.

"We'll, I'm dependent on a paycheck from that guy over there," and he pointed to the crew boss. "And you probably like your wooden furniture and all of the wood that makes your house, so don't act like we're bad guys." He responded, sounding a little more defensive than he liked.

"Lady, he's just doing his job, go complain to somebody else," Skeeter added, still unable to take his eyes off that hair.

"It's okay, the news people will be here soon, and then the public will know about this and I'll bet a lot of people around here will agree with us that these trees should be saved," she said, obviously not at all intimidated by them.

Skeeter figured she was one of those new people who immediately assumed that they knew what was best for everybody who lived on the island. He had lived a lifetime here, and his parents and grandparents before him, and he thought that they had done just fine without any help from outside. It was encounters such as this one that had led him to put that bumper sticker on his truck that Uncle Frank had brought back from a trip to Hawaii, that read: "We don't give a shit how you do it on the mainland."

Well, the meat needed stowing away in his freezer locker, and even if she was kind of nice to look at, this lady didn't look to be someone who would enjoy his company much, so Skeeter said goodbye to Guy (was that his name or was that just what all the drunken guys in the bar had called him?) and headed back to his truck, where someone who really liked his company waited.

They cruised on down the cove, through the dark, narrow canyon of fir trees that bordered Smugglers Cove Road. Rat Dog's head hung halfway out one open window, Skeeter leaned a bit toward the other slightly cracked window, a necessity due to the fumes from the leaky, rusted out tailpipe. The engine noise was enough that it startled an osprey out of her nest atop a big snag alongside the road. That actually bothered Skeeter some. Maybe he should do something about that muffler, at least for the wildlife's sake, if not his own. He squirmed in his seat, annoyed that the buckle of the seatbelt that he never bothered to use was digging into his butt. Yes, maybe, for the sake of the wildlife, he would try and patch the old muffler.

He detected a new noise over the roar of the engine, a sort of metallic clunking sound that turned out to be a can of Milwaukee's Best rolling around under the seat. With a little rummaging among the debris under the seat he succeeded in retrieving the can, and lifting his knees a bit he was able to use them to steady the wheel while his hands cracked open the can.

Life wasn't all bad, he thought, sipping the beer between gulps of the cold, biting air from the open window. They were barreling down the road at 50 plus mph through the narrow tunnel of foliage now. Occasionally there would be a brief glimpse of the Olympic Mountains to the right across Admiralty Inlet. Blue water and white mountain peaks under a grey canopy of cloud. Blink, it was there, blink, gone, then back a few moments later. The narrow asphalt two lane road bordered the crest of the 100 foot high sand-clay bank above the seashore. The roadway was set back maybe a hundred yards from the bank, following it for over a six mile stretch of the island's western coastline. A thick green fir, cedar, hemlock and spruce forest crowded in on both sides of the roadway. Elsewhere the power company had been pruning back trees along roadways like this one in order to reduce the damage to power lines from downed limbs or trees from windstorms. He enjoyed the fact that this stretch was still "unimproved."

After unloading the "lamb" at Sebering's, he thought, maybe, he and Rat Dog had earned a beer at the Doghouse, so they continued on down the island on the main highway another mile and turned left onto Coles Road, and followed that on into Langley and parked in front of the

Doghouse. He worried about running into Jack, but he decided that he wouldn't likely be waiting for him there at this hour. But if not today, no doubt he would find him sooner or later, so no point in trying too hard to avoid it. He wished that he could bring the old shotgun into the tavern with him, but that wasn't possible. So he again left it hidden away behind the driver's seat. Then he walked in, half bracing himself for a confrontation.

The tavern was almost empty at this hour. Jack must still be out in the woods cutting firewood. This didn't really relieve his mind, since all it did was delay the inevitable. It was early afternoon by then, so Skeeter had his usual pint of Rainier beer on tap, ordered some smoked salmon on sourdough bread and took his usual table in the back room with its fine view of Saratoga Passage out the east windows. He stared out at the clouds and surveyed the water between Camano and Whidbey Islands as he ate. The green, forested hump of Camano appeared gloomy and uninviting in the filtered light.

He knew that he should get his lazy butt off that chair and go out and get some wood cut so that he and Rat Dog could buy gas and food until some better work prospects opened up with the coming warmer weather. But he ordered another beer and rolled another cigarette and just sat there staring out at the cold, uninviting water of Saratoga Passage. Fuck it all, he repeated his "mantra."

A young woman who worked in the bar approached his table and asked if he wanted another beer, noticing that he had almost finished his. He stared down at the glass, a little fuzzy minded now. Should he? Then he looked up and saw Shelley, his girl friend from high school, who had dumped him not long after his so-called recovery from his war wounds.

"Workin' here now..." He mumbled, staring back down at his glass again. "Yeah, why not, sure, bring me another beer."

She frowned at his answer. Then she nodded and went off to get him another beer. 'I sure fucked that one up, didn't I,' he thought to himself as he remembered their break up last year. She was still as pretty as ever. Somebody was gonna get a sweet little wife there. But not Skeeter. She was ready to become little miss homemaker, with a cute little baby riding happily on her inviting, soft round hip.

She came back with the beer and silently set the glass down next to the empty one in front of him. Her eyes were a bit moist, but there was no hint of anything more than a lingering sadness at things that were beyond her power to change. 'Fuck it all,' Skeeter said to himself as he reached for the glass of beer, while deliberately keeping his eyes lowered to the foaming brew in front of him. She silently scooped up the empty glass and hurried away. Maybe he would get his midday meals and beer down at Cozy's in Clinton from now on.

After he finished the beer he walked a little wobblier than usual on out to the truck and an impatient Rat Dog. Once again they cruised on past the Moonraker Bookstore, Mike's and the marina and on up past the old school. But this time there was a Langley cop waiting to pull him over, just as he approached the fairgrounds.

"Aw, shit," he muttered as he pulled to a stop on the grassy shoulder of the road. The cop, an old school mate, got out of his car and walked up to the window of Skeeter's truck. Skeeter rolled down the window and smiled at Bud and nodded a greeting.

"Shit-faced, aren't you?" Bud asked the obviously rhetorical question of Skeeter, as he fixed a hard gaze on him.

"Yeah, well, I admit I had a couple beers with lunch, but I'm okay to drive. Got some wood to cut up over by Cultus Bay," Skeeter mumbled. "Nothin wrong with my driving is there?"

"Yeah, you're doing fine. But you know I should haul your sorry ass in right now for a breathalyzer test. But I won't, though don't expect me to let you off so easily next time. You know you're really asking for it, don't you? So get the hell out of here, and I hope you just cut one of your own legs off with that saw of yours instead of crippling or killing some innocent, unsuspecting driver on the way to the site."

Then he turned and walked back toward his car, as Skeeter muttered under his breath, "thanks, pig..." Part of him knew that the man had actually done him a favor, but Skeeter suddenly felt a terrible urge to pull the shotgun out from behind the seat and put a rifled slug into that smug, swaggering back as the cop returned to his car.

He got the truck running again after Bud had turned around and headed back into town. Then he took a left onto Sandy Point Road that eventually led him out to Wilkinson along the southern high bluff shoreline of the island, and then he proceeded on across the highway at the little "townlet" of Clinton and followed the shoreline until he eventually arrived at the site where he was still cutting firewood.

It scared him a little, the way a sudden rage could take hold of him at some imagined slight. Why did he do that? It was so fucked up to want to blow away the local cop who let him off with a little lecture instead of hauling him off to jail. Although with another DUI he had a good chance of losing his drivers license.

He pulled out his saw and a file and bar oil and fuel mix, but then he just sat there, staring out at the peaceful green that surrounded him, and out on the wide expanse of misty, steel blue of the water beyond the tree line. It might have been a source of solace to him at one time, but not today. Nothing seemed to help shake him out of his depression. Alcohol and drugs didn't seem to help. Nor did mingling with other people. He had a momentary flash of how easy it would be to get the shotgun out of the truck and how the shortened barrel would easily fit under his chin.

Instead of working that day, he decided that he would rather go fishing. So he and Rat Dog returned home and hauled his small rowboat out of the Blackberry patch that had grown up around it since the last time he had been out, the summer before. He drove on past the Greenbank Store and then made a sharp turn to the right at the bottom of the hill onto Wonn Road. It ended about a quarter mile to the east at the shoreline. There were about a hundred roads on the island that ended at the water, and according to law each one of them was a public beach access. But this time as Skeeter arrived at the end of Wonn Road to launch his small boat, he found that some guy had set a travel trailer at the road end.

Skeeter thought that was a little strange, but he started to unload the boat off the truck anyway. All of the sudden a guy burst out of the trailer door screaming his head off: "Get the hell out of here!"

When Skeeter said, "Whoa there, man, no reason to get all junkyard dog on me. So what's the story? Why can't I put my boat in here?"

This just made the guy even angrier. "You get the hell out of here right now, or I call the police!"

"Okay, you call the police. I don't think that they're gonna like what you're doin' man." Skeeter stood around waiting while the guy went in to call the cops. Then when they finally showed up, after having to put up with some real nastiness, Skeeter thought, 'Cool, now the cops will arrest this guy for harassment.'

But, no, they immediately went to Skeeter and wrestled him to the ground and put handcuffs on him. One of them grabbed him by the hair and dragged him over to the cop car and shoved him in. And he had ended up being hauled off to the county jail. He was eventually cut loose with the warning that next time he would be charged with criminal trespass on private property and get a $250 fine. Kind of unpleasant lesson about which law applies in a particular case. Seems that the other "golden rule" he'd heard about applied in this case. "He who has the gold, makes the rules." There were times when Skeeter wanted some payback so badly.

The local cops were in no mood to be gentle with suspects. Not too long ago two deputies had been gunned down by a mentally deranged suspect who managed to hide a pistol from them during an arrest. So a scruffy young guy like Skeeter was considered a potential threat to them, no matter if his offense was just jaywalking. He had never felt like such a stranger here in his own homeland as he did now. All of the sympathy for him as a wounded vet had long ago dried up and blown away. He was just considered one more loser, like Jack, who was a public nuisance, if not a public threat.

. . . .

The next day he packed everything he needed for the trip into Seattle into his beat up old pick up truck. The wiry, little mutt, trailing at his heels, leapt up into the passenger seat, and they made their way to the ferry dock and drove on to the next ferry on its way to the mainland.

The water was choppy and steel grey under an angry, dark sky that threatened to rain any moment. Skeeter, who was born in this wet land, didn't even bother to carry around a rain coat. Local folks just endured the wet. It rarely dumped on them, most often all it did was drizzle, and no one paid it that much mind. Yes, you got a little damp, but if you kept moving you could stave off the chill.

The twenty five minute crossing on the open deck ferry usually included some time in the small waiting room in a narrow cabin in the center of the boat. The occupants of the twenty some cars on board would congregate there and exchange bits of news and gossip. Today Skeeter didn't find anyone he knew there, so he just sat and watched the frothy waves in the inclement weather out the window. He sat and simply drew the salty sea breeze in and out of his nose, until the flat roof of Taylor's Landing, a seafood restaurant, finally appeared out of the mist, a sign of their arrival at the adjoining ferry dock.

He arrived at the Pike Place Market in downtown Seattle at about two in the afternoon. He was here to find a man who had told him that he would buy sacks of freshly cut salal from him for sale to florists. Maybe he had the wrong directions, but he couldn't seem to locate his vendor's stall in the market. Eventually, when he found someone who knew his way around the market to help him, he found the stall empty.

Hoping the owner might return later, Skeeter decided to hang out in a bookstore at the entrance to the market. As he opened the door and stepped into the small store, he thought, maybe, this wasn't such a good idea. Weird store. The shelves were filled with books and magazines that he had never seen elsewhere. Kind of troublemaking stuff. He browsed around a bit until he found a comic book on one shelf that caught his interest and he started reading it, sitting on a stool in one corner of the store.

With each page he read he was getting a little more pissed off. Was this the America that he had grown up in? It sure as hell didn't sound like it. The author, Howard Zinn, described an America with a long, ugly history of white supremacy and racism, a nasty place that went out of its way to keep Black people, Asians, Native Americans and even new European immigrant groups down. All of it serving the purposes of a small, privileged ruling elite, who profited from an ignorant, prejudiced population that couldn't see its own real interest.

He had never heard of such a thing as the military industrial complex either, declared such by no less an authority than President Dwight Eisenhower. He hadn't heard any of this, that is, until now, and already he could feel a growing uneasiness at his ignorance. It reminded him of that senseless war that had made his life such a mess.

He threw the comic book down, in disgust. 'Comic book? Ha, ha, very funny. What the hell kind of world was this, anyway? How could his dozen years of schooling have failed so miserably to tell him about shit like this? It just all seemed to make him feel a little crazier, reading stuff like this. He didn't need this. Fuck, no way.'

Chapter Three

After driving off the ferry after his trip to town, he took a left at the first
cross road and drove down toward his folk's place. After about a ten
minute drive down the narrow, winding country road, he arrived at the old
family farmstead. A new chill had settled over the land now that the sun
was again obscured by cloud cover. The typically cool, damp daytime low
forties air, moderated by slightly salt smelling breezes off the water, was
now falling back into the high thirties. If the sky cleared that evening it
might even drop into the low thirties and create a bit of frost again.

As he stacked the wood that his dad brought up from the barn with
the tractor into a storage bin near the door, he could smell the familiar
odors of a stew on the stove and the tang of alder woodsmoke in the air. It
was already lambing time, and there was the bleating of new-borns out in
the pasture and the responding calls of the mother ewes. In a few hours
they would be collecting in the barn for evening hay and protection from
predators.

There was a certain comfort to the old homestead, the forty odd
acres of mixed pasture, orchard and wood lot, and the ramshackle barn and
sheds and the weathered, old single story, clapboard farmhouse. There was
still a room in the back for him, but he hadn't lived here for over a year
now, ever since he'd regained enough of his health to be on his own. His
parents wanted to see him get out on his own, but even though they never
said much, he could tell that they didn't like how he lived.

Maybe he should try harder to get his shit together. But, to be
honest, he didn't feel like doing much of anything. What was the point,
after all? He was supposed to appreciate the fact that he had survived a war
that some friends and enough others had not, and now it was time to get on
with life. Since returning home he had convinced himself that he deserved
a chance to really enjoy a well-earned rest. Except he didn't seem to really
enjoy much of anything. He just did things, going through the motions, but
with little real care or interest. The VA doctor had wanted him to keep
popping pills, but their own family doctor had convinced him to quit taking
them. Maybe one less problem, but that was all it had been.

Whenever he would try to imagine life beyond what he had in his
isolated little shack out in the woods of central Whidbey, he couldn't get

past the thought that everything died, ended, crumbled into dust sooner or later, so why bother? Make more children who could then go off to die in the next war? And if the last war hadn't been ugly enough, there was the daily threat that our wise leaders, or maybe theirs, would fuck up and get us all fried in a nuclear war.

A lot of people still seemed to trust the folks in charge in this world a whole hell of a lot more than he did. He had seen, first hand, what could go wrong when you put your trust in your fellow man. Stupidity, arrogance, sadism, cowardice, betrayal, what weren't men capable of? Yes, on rare occasions one of them would rise above his lowly nature and do something noble and brave, but not often enough for his liking. Cruel land dwelling monkeys, that's all they were. Humanity wasn't worth a whole hell of a lot. Best to just steer clear of them, as much as possible. Fuck 'em!

He made an effort to keep his foul mouth under control at dinner with his folks that evening. He knew that that was one of the changes in him since his return from the war that they didn't like. That ranked right after their dislike of his drinking and his unwillingness to attend church with them any more. At least, they had the small satisfaction of his silent acceptance of the prayer that began their dinner, in which his dad never failed to include the provocative words: "...and may You watch over and guide our son, safely returned to us from the war, but still lost to your saving grace. Amen."

Then his dad brought up the subject he had dreaded, but knew it would be coming. "I heard that you've been spending a lot of time over at The Doghouse. That true?" His dad asked.

"Yeah..." He was getting pissed off now.

"And I heard that you had a little altercation in the parking in front of the tavern the other night with Jack's kid."

How did news travel so fast.? Even inaccurate news. "He just went a little crazy drunk on me, like he likes to do sometimes."

"And why would he do that?"

"Good question."

"We'll, you don't have to spend so much time around there, or with sorry people like Jack's boy. His father was never much fun to be around and it sounds like Jack junior isn't much better."

Skeeter nodded. That ended the topic, which was just fine with Skeeter.

That evening as he and Rat Dog cruised back north to Greenbank, as they passed South Whidbey Sate Park he noticed a little VW bug parked in the park's lot adjacent to Smugglers Cove Road. And then he saw a light, a small lantern off through the trees across the road, in the forest scheduled for cutting. It roused his curiosity enough to cause him to cut his lights and his engine and coast to a stop in a space near the car.

He quietly exited the cab and slipped into the woods. He knew how to silently stalk prey from a lifetime in the woods, as a hunter, and the army had taught him a few things about how to survive in the jungle against the deadliest predator of all, his fellow man. Or at least they had tried. He slowly made his way down a forest path that he thought the others had followed, using only his night vision to pick out the trail, while carefully avoiding fallen branches that could make any noise.

He came to a fork in the trail and stopped. Which way to turn? Then he felt something brush against his leg, which caused a momentary rush of adrenaline and for his heart to race. Then he heard a faint whimper. It was Rat Dog, who must have squeezed through the partly opened truck window. And then the dog chose one fork of the trail and scrambled on ahead. Skeeter followed.

About five minutes later he and the dog could see a dim light glowing through the brush and they could hear voices. "So should the nail go straight in to the tree or at an angle? And how high up from the ground should it be?"

Tree spiking! The assholes, Skeeter fumed to himself. And the next thing he knew, he was shouting it aloud: "You assholes!"

"Hey, who's that?" A voice called out, followed by muffled voices and a scrambling to find cover in the thick understory.

Skeeter and Rat Dog stepped into a small clearing where a bag of nails and a hammer lay at the base of a big Douglas fir. Skeeter flipped the switch on his flashlight and swept the light over the scene and off into the surrounding brush. "This is just plain stupid," he shouted. "Anybody cutting that tree or milling the logs later risks getting hurt by chunks of flying metal. And you could end up with some serious jail time, not to mention making some enemies you really don't want. Assholes."

Several heads poked out of the salmon berry and salal undergrowth. The group from the Doghouse emerged from the dark and stood a bit hang dog in front of him. Young people in wool sweaters and stocking caps, three men and two women, one of them his red haired "friend," looked at him anxiously, unsure of what was to come next.

Then a police siren suddenly shrieked and a blue flashing light penetrated the foliage to where they stood. A voice on a speaker system announced: "whoever is in there, show yourself now!"

"You turning us in?" Asked one of the young guys.

"I should," he said, as he considered his options. It would certainly serve them right, he thought to himself. But how do I convince the cops that I wasn't part of this? He was not one of the most popular people with the local constabulary. It would be hard to get them to believe that he was just a good citizen, stopped to do his civic duty and stop a crime in progress. Fuck it. I don't owe the cops any favors. Let them catch these guys in the act, he decided, and said, "but I won't. But I'm out of here. The cops are your problem." And he called Rat Dog to him, and the two of them darted off down a trail deeper into the forest.

The others stood there, momentarily confused. Then one of them said, "Come on, he and his dog know these trails. Follow them." And he and Rat Dog could hear the whole group pounding down the trail after them.

Skeeter tried to quicken his pace, hoping to lose them. Then he jogged to the left as another spur off the main trail appeared in front of him. He turned off his light and began to feel his way along the new trail just using his feet to guide him. It looked like he had succeeded in ditching them. But then he could hear their voices. "No, he didn't go that way. He turned off back at that side trail behind us."

"Oh, shit," he said. 'They really are following me! I don't need this shit. That's what I get for poking my nose into business that has nothing to do with me. Why didn't I just keep going when I had the chance?' "Shit," he fumed, as he flicked the flashlight back on and he and the dog tried to put more distance between them and their pursuers.

The thick forest duff in the old growth mixed fir, cedar and spruce forest created a spongy carpet under their feet as they ran. The six to eight foot wide tree trunks flickered in his light as he passed them by. The flashlight illuminated the reddish brown trunks of the Douglas firs with their deep grooves where sections of the thick, rough bark had separated as the trees grew wider over the years. The gray bark of the spruces had a kind of scaly, cornflake look, while the long, narrow striations of the gray brown cedar bark appeared smooth and soft in the flashlight glow. There was a slight hint of cedar scent in the cool, moist air, and a spotted owl hooted to a mate somewhere far off in the dark treetops.

They eventually passed out of the old growth and into a second growth forest of mixed alder, hemlock and fir. Here the forest floor was solider as the heavy needle duff was replaced by a heavy clay with a thin layer of alder leaves and hemlock needles. The air was drier and colder and there was more light from the gray night sky.

About a half hour later and maybe two miles distance, he and his dog approached his small cabin. Skeeter pushed the door open and led the way in. He lit a kerosene lamp and as the others approached the door, he slammed it shut in their faces.

He could hear them, standing outside in the chill, damp dark talking in hushed voices among themselves. "Let's just leave this jerk here, and find our way out of here on our own"

"Oh, you think that's gonna be so easy. Do you know where we are? I don't have a clue."

"Oh, fuck it," Skeeter finally said to himself. Then he opened the door and said, "Come on in, assholes."

They hesitated, but then considered their options, and entered. He invited them to sit around the table on the few chairs and some overturned buckets, as he gathered some kindling and several split pieces of firewood and placed them in the wood stove and lit the fire with a piece of newspaper he lit with a match.

His guests peered around the room a bit in disbelief. On one wall there was a set of pegs with various fishing gear, nets, crab pots and the like hanging from them. Logging equipment, a splitting mall, a hand winch, some lengths of steel cable, saws and an axe rested against another wall. There was a bookshelf behind the bed with books on truck repair, hunting, and the like, and there was also a set of old Readers Digest Magazines with a few National Geographic Magazines mixed in. They were less impressed by the beer cans scattered all over the floor and the dirty clothes that lay in a pile in one corner. And the evident signs that no one had swept cobwebs or cleaned a window in years. Once they were all settled and a pot was boiling on the stove for tea, Skeeter broke the ice.

"You know, local people like to call you swamp hippies. Sort of creepy people who hang out in dark, swampy woods and come out once in a while to cause some trouble."

The red haired girl reacted first. "Ignorant people say and do a lot of things. Draining marshlands or filling them in, as if they were just wasteland, instead of valuable wildlife habitat. Those are the kidneys of the earth that filter water before returning it to the streams. Where do you think the salmon get clean water to spawn in?"

"Okay, so maybe you know a thing or two about ecology that some of the old timers around here don't. But you tell people they're stupid and that everything they know and do is wrong and then you're surprised when they say, fuck you."

She looked around a bit and muttered, "what a pig sty."

"Fuck you," Skeeter shot back.

"Hey," said a long haired guy in a colorful wool cap. "Let's start over. My name is Ross, this is Hal and Carl, and he pointed to a short young guy with granny glasses and a peach fuzz blond beard, and a dark, lean young man with a green down vest and green army fatigues, both of whom nodded. "And this is Annie," pointing to a short chestnut haired young woman in a black wool pea coat. "And this is "Austin," and he gestured toward the red haired girl. "Bet you could never guess where she's from," he smiled.

"Texas," she said. "And from a mighty nice town out there."

Now he could hear the bit of Texas in her voice. "Okay. And I'm known as Skeeter," he answered.

There were a few smirks shared among them as they heard his name. "Thanks, man, for not turning us in to the cops," said Ross. "But, man, don't you think our cause is a righteous one?"

"Maybe, maybe not," he replied.

"So you don't like spiking..."

"Not so much."

"Well, dozens more trees would be down by now if we hadn't blocked the work today. And it may buy time for some political wrangling in Olympia to get some government action. They're logging public land, after all, and right next to a state park. The last stand of old growth on South Whidbey," said Austin, her eyes blazing.

"Yeah," said Skeeter. "Very stupid, spiking trees, but I have to admit that there is plenty of hundred year old second growth forest around here, no need to log off the last big old trees on the south end."

"So, take sides..." She said, now eyeing him with a penetrating gaze that was beginning to have an effect.

"Seems like I have, to some extent already, saving your sorry asses."

"So now what?" She asked.

"Lay low til morning, wait them out, and then go back for your car early, before the cops come back from their donuts and coffee."

The kettle boiled and Skeeter searched up a few cups and some small canning jars and filled them with black tea brewed in the kettle. Then he toasted some Wonder Bread on the wood stove. As he handed it out, there was a polite nod and muttered 'thank you,' but it obviously wasn't their favorite food. Ross finally broke the silence with, "did you ever hear the one about the logger who made moose turd pie?" The others groaned, but Ross pushed on: "There was a new logger in a camp who was told that the new guy had to cook for everybody, unless somebody complained, in which case that person had to do the cooking. So the new logger went out in the woods and found the biggest moose turd he could find and baked it into a pie. Then he served it with supper that night. And after the meal the biggest, meanest logger on the crew sat down and cut into the pie and took the first slice. When he bit into his first mouthful of pie, he stopped. Then he slammed his fork down on the table and looked around, and with the meanest glare anyone had ever seen, he shouted: "My God! That's moose turd pie!" Then, after moment to think, he muttered, "but it's good."

They all laughed, even though they had heard it before, and Skeeter laughed too. Then others started telling their own jokes and Skeeter laughed more than he had in a very long time.

The moon rose and its light revealed delicate patterns outlined in the frost on the window pane. Austin, who was seated near the window, studied the lovely white shapes formed by the ice crystals. It wasn't the first time that the ice had formed into such patterns on his little window, but it was the first time that Skeeter had ever noticed it. What he had actually noticed was the young woman next to him at the small table, and somehow that had drawn his attention to what she was paying attention to.

About then she noticed him watching what she was looking at. "Pretty, isn't it," she said.

Skeeter nodded and then yawned. "Here," he said, "are some old blankets and a quilt my mom made. And there's a jacket or two and some cushions over there. You can make up a bit of bedding with all this. Get a little sleep yet before dawn." And he dimmed the wick on the oil lamp and went off to curl up on his own small bed. The others improvised their own bedding as best they could, and then eventually all of the voices faded, as ears shut down, and one by one they each surrendered to sleep.

Chapter Four

Skeeter woke during the night in a panic. He reached for the shotgun, but it wasn't there. Then he spied the several dozing forms around him in the cabin. Ross was curled up on the rug in front of the wood-stove. Austin lay in the arm chair with Rat Dog curled up in her lap. The others had found blankets or cushions to lay on the floor. Being surrounded by all of these other beings was strangely comforting, and he rolled back over and fell asleep.

The next morning he was the first one up. He climbed out of his bed in the small loft and slipped outside to pee. He couldn't remember a night when he had slept so soundly, if only for a few hours, without interruption. He had hardly seemed to miss the usual comforting feel of the shotgun resting against his hip in bed either. He'd left it back in the truck.

When he returned, the others had begun to rouse themselves with the approach of dawn, urged along by the faint chatter of bird song that grew stronger with the increasing light. Skeeter boiled up some coffee for them, and they filled up on toast. They were all a bit subdued this morning. No one had much to say. Maybe the strangeness of being back in the woods in an unfamiliar place with a strange guy they barely knew had caught up with them. Skeeter actually welcomed the silence. He was more familiar with that than all of the chatter of the night before.

He eventually suggested that they take a walk back to their car by way of a backwoods trail he knew. He guided them along a trail that led them north through an aging second growth forest of towering alder trees, many nearly three feet in diameter and easily 150 feet tall after some ninety years of life. The bare branched deciduous alders, with their nitrogen fixing roots, fed a smaller understory forest of conifers; hemlocks, firs, spruce and cedar that would some day replace the pioneer alders to once again become the climax forest of woodland giants that had once graced this site.

There was still plenty of evidence of the old growth fir forest the second growth had replaced. Giant old stumps, six feet tall and some seven feet across, with notching for the sawyers' platforms, were scattered every hundred feet or so throughout the forest. Many of the old logs lay where they fell, the loggers so sated by the over abundance of timber that they only chose to select out the biggest and best logs to haul out of the woods, in an old practice known as hi-grading. The work was done with the help of steel cables attached to powerful steam driven haulers known as donkey engines,

No one spoke until Skeeter led them out to a promontory looking out on Admiralty Inlet, two hundred feet above the Sound. From where they stood near the edge of the clay, sand and gravel high bank they could see ten miles across the water, where the hundred year old city of Port Townsend perched on the Olympic Peninsula at the head of the Straits of Juan de Fuca, a wide strait that led out to the Pacific Ocean some hundred miles beyond. They were too far away to make out the century old two and three story Victorian era brick buildings that comprised the several block long downtown. Dreamers and schemers had invested heavily in the city a century ago in the belief that the railroad would push its way up Hood Canal on the east side of the Olympic Peninsula and make Port Townsend a major West Coast seaport. The railroad never came, and the city never grew beyond its initial three block downtown and twenty odd uphill streets of modest salt box houses and the occasional Victorian mansion.

A plume of white smoke rose up from the pulp mill just north of town and the snow-clad Olympic Mountains formed a hundred mile wall as a majestic back drop to the town. It was at that moment that a long, dark steel gray form emerged from the thin mist out of the mouth of Hood Canal to the south of town. It was one of the mammoth Trident nuclear submarines based on the Canal.

The group of them watched the sub in hushed silence. It was a sinister reminder that this was Ground Zero in the event of a nuclear war, and long after all of them were incinerated ash, there would still be such submarines somewhere out in the Pacific pointlessly poised to retaliate, each sub equipped with enough long range missiles with nuclear warheads to destroy hundreds of Soviet cities.

The small group of young people gathered on the bluff looking out on this scene had never known a day in their lives when the threat of nuclear annihilation had not hung like a Damoclean sword over their heads. It colored and conditioned their lives in subtle and often unconscious ways that no previous generation of Americans had ever known. They had nightmares of sudden catastrophe. They took foolish risks in their daily lives and lived in the moment in ways that their depression era, security conscious parents struggled to understand.

The frosty morning air carried a sweet smell of saltwater. The early morning sun in the east cast a rosy mauve glow across the white peaks of the Olympic Mountains to the west. If the Trident sub cast a momentary pall over their morning, it was overwhelmed by the sheer magnificence of the vast panorama of water and mountain that lay before them. Skeeter drew the cold maritime air into his lungs, a deep, full breath of the sweet clean breeze that had flowed off the ocean through the long trough of the Strait of Juan de Fuca. All in all, still a good day to be alive, he thought to himself.

His companions were in similarly good spirits as they gazed upon the scene and basked in the rising sun and felt the cool, sea fresh breeze on their faces. Skeeter looked back landward and saw the ashes of an old house fire that brought a momentary chill as the memories flooded back. Not too long ago he and his fellow crew of local volunteer firefighters had been called to the site, not to put out the blaze, but to keep the ashes from flaring up after the house on the site had burned to the ground.

A group of white supremacists had ended a violent crime spree on this very spot not so long ago. After killing a Jewish talk show host in Colorado, the gang had gone on to Portland, Oregon where they had robbed a bank and wounded a security guard in the process. Then they had fled to the island and rented the house on this site, convinced that it would be a great place to hide out from the authorities.

What they hadn't counted on was what a small, nosy community they had really landed in. Within a week everyone down at the Greenbank Store knew they were Neo-nazi cut throats. The government sent in SWAT teams that surrounded the house and all but the leader of the gang gave themselves up. He decided to shoot it out with them. And after a cold, wet, windy December day and night of sporadic gunfire that echoed over several square miles of Greenbank, the volunteer fire department had received the call to come on over to the site with the fire truck, that there was going to be a fire, and they would be needed to put it out.

The news that evening reported that a flare fired into the house had ignited the tinder dry cedar structure and set it ablaze. The fire crew wasn't called in to "fight" the blaze until it had pretty much burned itself out.

When Skeeter and his crew mates were eventually let in to the scene, there was just a layer of smoldering ash left, and in the middle of the ash heap there was a charred skeleton and a bare rifle barrel, all the wood burned away from it.

The larger scene around the site was equally eerie, there were trenches dug a distance from the building all around the perimeter of the structure, littered with fast food wrappers and spent rifle cartridges. As he recalled the scene that night, he decided not to say anything to his companions, let them imagine that they were basking in some pristine corner of nature. Private citizen crazy violence could be pretty ugly, but government sponsored violence could trump it all.

Not that nature was all that non-violent, but it had trouble matching the sheer scale and ferocity of human violence: the mountain of skulls that Genghis Khan had created in Persia in the course of his conquests. The ovens of the Nazi concentration camps that incinerated millions of men, women and children. The firestorms over Dresden and other German cities created by incendiary bombs. The nuclear destruction of the Japanese cities of Hiroshima and Nagasaki. And everywhere he looked there seemed to be evidence of human violence, such as the ash heap near where they stood, or the violence that the former naval bombing range two miles north of there at Lake Hancock represented. It had been a number of years since navy planes had used the 400 acres of the beautiful saltwater lagoon for bombing practice, but it was still deemed unsafe to enter the area, with a continued risk of accidentally setting off unexploded ordinance buried in the ground there.

And a trip to the bar was always a good reminder of how much pent up violence, frustration and anger lay just below the surface in his world. Too many men who came back from war seemed to end up in jail, on the streets, or dead. No ones fault but their own? But it scared Skeeter, that anger that occasionally caught fire. It could flare up at any time, but often it seemed directed against those who didn't understand or give a damn about what he had been through over there.

Too much doom and gloom for a day when the beauty of the world shone like a beacon on this bluff overlooking the ocean. Ross had lit a joint by then and he was passing it around among his friends. Skeeter took a hit and knew immediately that it was an inferior grade, nothing like the stuff he grew in pots atop the big old stumps in his woods. But it seemed to lend a further bit of sharpness to the colors of that "outer magnificence" as one nature poet had described it.

He sat back and just watched it all go by for a while. The clouds, the dappled sunlight on the long, red gold tresses of the young woman perched on the bluff edge in front of him. Whoa! He'd just noticed that Hal and Carl were holding hands. What the fuck, a couple of queers, and they didn't even have the decency to hide it. "I'm outta here. Just back track to the road and follow it south for a couple of miles and you're back to your car. See ya around."

"What about your truck, man?" Asked Ross.
"I'll go get it. Don't worry about it, man. See you around." And Skeeter hurried off.

Skeeter returned to his truck and headed home again, where he and Rat Dog prepared to catch up on their sleep. He was hungry by then, so he pulled a carton of milk out of the metal cold box built into the north wall of the house and poured himself a glass. There was no electricity in the cabin, but for about eight months of the year, things like milk and cheese remained relatively cool to cold in the cold box, with its metal back exposed to the outside air on the shaded backside of the house, since daytime temperatures in the shade rarely rose above 50 degrees and night time often hovered in the low forties or high thirties, rarely dropping below freezing. The Maritime Pacific Northwest was often chilly, but rarely a cold place. The climate was so mild that many older houses in this part of the country didn't even have insulation in the walls, the owners thought it was enough to just have a sealed airspace between sets of inner and outer wall boards.

He didn't have a well either, just a rain barrel that collected water off the roof for washing. He hauled in five gallon containers of drinking water. And his lighting came from kerosene lamps. Maybe there weren't that many Americans still living like that anymore in the1970's, but less than a century ago many, if not most people on the island had.

After he'd downed the glass of milk he rummaged around looking for more shells for his old twenty gauge Eastern Arms shot gun with its slightly shortened barrel to scatter the shot a bit. He found a box of shells, He considered whether loading the gun with buck shot would be a good idea, but he decided to go with the bird shot. Less chance that he might do some real harm. Enough to just scare them away. Who, he wasn't sure. Jack, for sure, but there were others he couldn't name, but he knew there were others out to get him.

What was this thing with Jack? Would he just keep escalating things, push him? After all, he'd been letting it all just go by, without any response. Shouldn't the bastard let up on him? But he somehow knew he wouldn't. God, how he would love to just put a bullet through that nasty fucker's brain.

He pulled off his clothes, down to his long johns, climbed up into the loft, where he lay back in bed to rest a while, with Rat Dog nuzzled into one arm pit and with the shot gun resting along his other side within easy reach. The clouds had moved back in, the upper reaches of the room lay in the shadows, and a patter of light rain was just audible on the cabin roof above his head.

'Shit,' he thought. 'What a fuck up I am. Why did I let myself be humiliated by that nasty bastard again the other night? And now he was feeling even angrier at himself and a bit scared. Wouldn't it feel good to just waste that son of bitch? But what a waste to go do jail time for wasting a turd like Jack. I need to get a life, he thought to himself. So does he. I'm just spending too much of my time thinking about that prick. What kind of a life is that? But I've just been minding my own business when he starts messing with me. But then, what other choice do I really have than to put up with his shit. I have to keep my head and think it through...'

Impulsive actions seemed to be among the most regrettable. Which now included his decision to aid and abet the tree huggers, who would have probably landed their sorry asses in jail for tree spiking if he hadn't come along when he did. Though they seemed likable enough, not out to hurt anyone, really, not like Jack. But queers? ... He didn't even want to think about what those perverts did with each other. It was just too gross. He should have just left the fucking hippies alone. He was such a fuck up. Really... He thought as his mind drifted off into a sound sleep.

Oddly, Skeeter was in his sixty fifth year, and he was still in retreat in the small, tumble down shack in the woods near Greenbank. He still had himself a dog. This one though, was a bigger, tougher version of his old Rat Dog. But he and the dog had continued the crusty old bachelor's life.

He was even more reclusive these days, almost a hermit. His parents were both dead and their farm sold to a gentleman horse rancher. He didn't have any friends. He did have a hobby though.

He would spend his days driving the island roads with his dog and his fishing gear, checking out various accesses for casting for salmon from the shore. That was more difficult now that all of the public accesses had been taken over by wealthy beach owners. What no one knew though, was that Skeeter didn't give a damn about fishing. He was spending all his time scouting the big mansions that a new class of billionaires were building along the coastline of the island. Much to his astonishment the island had become a favorite location for summer homes for those who had become super rich. These were men who had grown incredibly wealthy off the lucrative healthcare trade, the booming oil and electronic industries, private prisons and the always booming military production, and they all took advantage of overseas sweatshop labor. They built huge mansions on large estates overlooking the Sound. Some had even built on former beachfront state parks that an impoverished state had felt compelled to sell off. They would often, in addition to having access to their yachts anchored out in the water below their homes, also create helipads that would allow them to come and go at ease from their estates, with no need to endure the traffic jams and ferry line back ups that increasingly plagued the ordinary people of the region.

Skeeter apparently did not admire the achievements of these giants of industry the way most of his fellows did. And now that he was old, he no longer feared them either. "When you got nothin, you got nothin to lose." That's how Skeeter felt these days. And who would suspect a scruffy old guy in a beat up old pick up truck with a mangy dog and a second rate fishing pole of any serious mischief.

But serious mischief did occur with increasing frequency on the island. Beautiful twenty five room, three story mansions would mysteriously be torched in the middle of a winter's night, when owners were off enjoying the warm, sunny Caribbean, and caretakers were tucked into their beds in some modest bungalow miles from the estate. Skeeter would scout a place for months before taking action, and he favored cold, wet winter nights when the fires would be less likely to spread to the surrounding forest.

He was quite patient and methodical about the whole business. He had spent hours carefully experimenting at home with combustible mixtures in order to come up with just the right formula for a hot, long lasting fire from the Molotov cocktails that he would hurl through windows that he had first punched out with a specially designed metal rod.

Burglar alarms didn't matter a whit to him. He didn't want to enter the houses and roam around anyway. All he needed was a couple of minutes to smash a window and deliver the goods. He was usually long gone by the time police cars were able to arrive at the usually quite remote estates. And, in fact, he really didn't give much of a damn if they did eventually catch him. So what? He was old and tired, and mostly disinterested in life. All it was was a little hobby he had settled on in his solitary senior years, that just happened to hark back to an earlier time in his life, when he also thought he had nothing to lose.

Of course, criminals who can't resist repeating their crimes do eventually get caught. Skeeter was no exception. All of the smoldering crime scenes, carefully sifted over by an army of investigators, did eventually yield a result. And the evidence pointed directly at an old codger living in a little shack out in a forest not far from South Whidbey State Park.

One morning after a night of mischief Skeeter woke to the sound of a bullhorn announcing that his little shack was surrounded by law enforcement agents, and he would be best advised to give himself up peacefully. That was the moment that Skeeter awoke with a start from the strange dream. What was it he had dreamed? Really weird shit. Where did it come from? It kind of scared him. But had he dreamed that someone was near the house, stalking him? It wouldn't surprise him if there really was someone out there.

But now that he was fully awake, he could tell by the bird activity outside the cabin that nothing was snooping around. A flock of juncoes were chattering away, while encircling the suet block next to the house and taking turns launching themselves from nearby branches onto the hanging block, with a couple of black capped chickadees waiting in the wings, so to speak, flitting in and out of the branches of the nearby red elderberry bushes. A plump little gray brown fox sparrow also hovered nearby, while an even smaller brown winter wren skittered along the outside walls of the cabin. And he and his dog were still comfortably tucked into bed.

He pulled the shotgun up alongside him. It wouldn't be that hard to get the end of the barrel under his chin while reaching down and pulling the trigger. He stared at the walls of the cabin. Had he dreamed the whole thing last night, the visitors, as well? But there was the proof in scattered bedding and dirty cups.

A week passed. He awoke that morning as usual, after another restless night filled with bad dreams and night terrors, feeling tired and anxious. He paced the cabin restlessly and aimlessly, as if he were trapped in a prison cell, until he could stand it no more. Then he grabbed his shotgun and called Rat Dog, and they set off on foot into the forest behind the cabin. A half hour later they were in the 200 acre grove of old growth fir, spruce and cedar adjoining the state park. It was his first time back there since the night with the hippies.

He wondered what they were up to. Yeah, they were naive jerks, tree spiking. What assholes. But he had to admit that it would be a shame if the trees were harvested. The 300 to perhaps even 600 or more year old trees stood tall and majestic above them. Walking amidst the six to nine foot diameter tree trunks made him feel like some forest imp or dwarf, and looking up some 200 feet into the dappled sunlight of the forest canopy was almost like gazing up into the high ceiling of a grand cathedral. Yes, he realized that the awe he felt was truly akin to that. The walk across the soft, deep, spongy moss carpet under his feet, beneath the lofty, majestic, green vault of tree crowns high above his head, was a walk through a sacred cathedral of nature's own making.

Later that day when the dog and man arrived back at the cabin after a good hike in the woods, he found a note on the windshield of his truck from Ross, inviting him over to their place for supper that night. A kind of thank you for his putting them up. It included directions and suggested he try to get there before dark. Since darkness came early, between five and six in the early evening in March this far north, it was nearly late enough in the day for him to start on over if he wanted to take them up on the offer.

It wasn't like he had a crowded social calendar, but the queer guys would be there... Well, so what, he thought. Gays, he'd heard, was the term they preferred. Now if they were lesbians that wouldn't be so bad. He could get himself to imagine what they did together, and the vision actually drew him to kind of want to watch. I guess that was why porn movies liked to show scenes of two women getting it on at times.

He peered nervously around him. If Ross could come back in and leave a note for him so easily, other people could come back in here as well. They could be watching him right now. If they had spotted Skeeter's truck earlier, they might be sitting somewhere just out of sight, laying in wait for him to show up. It was wearing on his nerves. There could be a rifle scope trained on him at this very moment, following his every move as he climbed into the truck. He half expected to hear the crack of a rifle shot any moment now. But it never came, and he considered going out after all.

The drive out made him feel as if he had been given some small, temporary reprieve from the deadly threat that lay over him every day. So he would go have supper with the Nature Kids, as he decided to call them. Fuck it, man. As if he needed to please anyone by staying away from the newcomers. His people... What the hell was that, anyway? So he drew the flaps down on his hat and opened the windows on both sides so a good strong breeze would blow through the cab. Maybe he'd go visit the friendly guy just outside of Langley with the two dozen old wrecked cars in his backwoods, and see if maybe one of the mufflers would fit on the truck.

He glanced over at Rat Dog as he took up his usual perch out the passenger side window as he fired up the engine. It was a wonder he hadn't lost the mutt out the window by now, he thought to himself as the limber little dog stretched his neck and shoulders as far out the window as he could without tumbling out. "Don't push your luck now, pal," he said to the dog.

A chilly dog and man eventually stumbled out of the truck at the old farmhouse on a back road just south of the town of Freeland. They both trembled a bit trying to get some circulation going to counteract the cold that had settled in their bones. They weren't quite candidates for hypothermia yet, but a warm stove and a hot drink would be welcome.

The aging white farmhouse was familiar to Skeeter with its weathered gray outbuildings and lichen encrusted old orchard of yellow transparent, gravenstein and king apples, among the most common varieties that settlers had grown that didn't easily succumb to fungal diseases in the damp maritime Northwest. Until a few years ago this place had belonged to an old couple, who had raised their kids here. Like a number of old homesteads on south Whidbey it had never served the settlers particularly well. They had been lured here early in the century by real estate brochures that promised prime farm land once the big tree stumps were removed. After all, as the sales pitch went, the land must be fertile or how could it have produced such huge trees. But, in fact, the land was mainly glacial till here, a combination of sand, clay and gravel in seemingly random layers cast about by the great glaciers that had covered the land some ten thousand years ago.

It could produce great trees, but the soil was thin. It was often highly acidic from the predominance of conifers, and the forest duff hid a thin layer of topsoil that was readily depleted by most crops grown in it. Some fruit trees and berry crops might do passably well, and pasture grass could be adequate to raise a few dairy or meat animals, but even that was predicated on the removal of deep rooted, mammoth stumps that were everywhere on the landscape. So no one had ever prospered as a farmer on the south end of the island. Nearly everyone there had to do some work out, on boats or in the woods or in the mills, and to harvest local venison and wild salmon during the seasons to supplement their diet.

The Coupeville prairie, of course, was the exception. The local native people had been burning off the prairie and managing a population of camas, nettle and fern there as food sources for hundreds, perhaps, even thousands of years. The forests had been left mostly undisturbed. For the native people it was a source of wood for various uses, including some big trees for totem pole, home and boat construction. But these uses had barely made a dent in the vast old growth forests of the region.

The biggest joke on the settlers was Freeland. Back in the early 20th century an idealistic group of utopian socialists had created a small community at the end of Holmes Harbor that they had named Freeland. The name derived from their ambition that like-minded settlers could come get started on freely given, modest plots of land where they would have the opportunity to prosper within the progressive community. However, they soon joined the majority of the southend's population, just getting by on whatever work they could find in addition to the meager production of their mini-farms. They soon blended into the larger community, their radical past buried away. And now here was a new wave of naive, young idealists come to try their luck as the latest generation yearning to be free, as they made their way "back to the land."

Skeeter felt a bit awkward at first, as he stepped up to the door and knocked. He wasn't so sure he belonged here. Nor was he at all sure why he had even been invited over. He barely knew these people, and they knew nothing about him. And maybe the more they knew, the less they would want him around.

There was no hesitation, however, by the person who answered the door. Carl gave Skeeter and his dog a welcoming smile and invited them in. The others were there, and Ross immediately stepped up and shook his hand. The women were a bit more standoffish. When Carl gave him a little hug, Skeeter stood there kind of limply, enduring it, while trying not to show any distaste.

He was also uncomfortable when the group of them sat down to eat supper, because before beginning, they took each other's hands and held them in a silent circle that included Skeeter. It went on for what seemed like an eternity, and he just held his breath and tried not to tense up too much. Who the fuck were these people? Some airy fairy crew? And what was he doing here with them?

The vegetarian chili he ate that evening was a little weird too. But Rat Dog seemed to enjoy the small bowl they gave him, and now lay at their feet, snoring contentedly. He was even less impressed by Austin's sales pitch. "This recipe came from Francis Moore Lappe's cookbook, *Diet for a Small Planet*," she explained. "The author tells how there would be plenty enough food for everyone if we just quit eating meat. Combinations of grains and beans and vegetables can be healthy and nourishing and Indian people of the Americas learned long ago how to live on them."

He wasn't quite so sure that native people of the coastal Pacific Northwest would agree. Seafood had sustained them for thousands of years, with the modest addition of starch from camas bulbs and cattail root and a few wild greens and a berry crop. Securing food was so easy on Puget Sound, with its clams, mussels, salmon and other sea creatures in such abundance, that they liked to say that "only a fool could starve to death on Puget Sound." The early white settlers, who had come from agricultural communities and had hoped to prosper in the same way in this new land, may not have gone hungry, but too many of them had worn themselves out trying to make a go at farming the south end of the island's infertile glacial till.

All the same, Skeeter couldn't bring himself to contradict her if it meant that he would have to leave here without getting a full portion of gazing into those green eyes set in a pale, freckled face surrounded by the loveliest red gold hair he had ever seen. Oh yes, he was smitten.

He tried not to be too obvious though. She didn't seem all that impressed by him, in any event. He glanced down at his dirty fingernails, and then he self-consciously tried to hide them below the table top. He also began to wonder if he had trimmed his beard or hair recently. At least he had done a laundry last week, and he was wearing a clean, if slightly ragged, flannel shirt tonight.

The low point of the evening came when Ross made a crack about the loggers. "A bunch of low life losers with bad teeth and no permanent address." The others chortled at his witty comment, but Skeeter wasn't amused. How many of his family, parents, aunts and uncles, had managed to keep many teeth. They had been raised in harder times when the right foods and proper dental care, if any, were beyond them. But they made sure that their kids had better. It shamed him a bit, but it mostly pissed him off, thinking about how rural folk of Island County still bore some of the scars of rural hard living that young, pampered city kids could laugh at.

"Yep, you and me, Ross," Skeeter said. "We are the only cool guys, except sometimes I'm not so sure about you, good buddy ". Ross's face drooped a little as the words sunk in. Maybe time to go, thought Skeeter.

"Hey, how about a little weed, man?" Suggested Ross as he filled a pipe with some marijuana. Skeeter thought that wouldn't be so bad. He took a few tokes as the pipe got passed around the room.

As the hallucinogen in the herb began to take effect, he started to focus on little things around him. There was the music, some Andean pan pipes, playing on a record player in the room. Then he noticed a comic book on a little table next to his chair. It was an R. Crumb comic, with outrageous cartoon figures, with provocative dialogue. Crude jokes and subtle and not so subtle mockery of things like racism and sexism. Then he read a cartoon story that he found hilarious. It followed the story of a flock of chickens who are set free by their keeper. The story line was narrated in Doctor Seuss-like nursery rhyme fashion. "There were chickens riding Cadillacs to Washington D.C./ The day I set my chickens free..." Yeah, set those chickens free, Skeeter laughed as he studied the picture of a bunch of chickens riding in an open Cadillac convertible.

He was still smiling as he stood up and announced to the others, "time I was going home. Thanks for the invite."

"Hey, man, come back whenever you like. You're always welcome here," said Ross as he followed Skeeter as he made his way to the door. Austin gave him a little pat on the shoulder, and one of the gay boys offered him another light hug, at which Skeeter tried not to show any obvious displeasure.

He returned to the truck with Rat Dog trailing behind, a little more reluctant to leave than Skeeter, with everyone lavishing attention on him. Spoiling him, thought Skeeter, who gave him a gentle little kick up into the cab with his foot.

Skeeter drove more carefully this evening. It helped that he was only a bit stoned and not drunk. The air had turned crisp and cold as the sky cleared and a million stars glittered in the black roof of night above their heads. Only to the south was there a faint glow of artificial light from the mainland. Each year that light grew stronger as the population of the Puget Sound basin, stretching from Olympia in the south to Everett in the north with Tacoma and Seattle in between continued to increase. It was clear that the several cities would someday sprawl to such an extent that Pugetopolis, as it was increasingly being called, would be an apt name for it all.

Chapter Five

Skeeter was feeling a little down after the visit to the Nature Kids. Their lives looked so much better than his own, that spending time with them only made him feel worse about his own life. They had a kind of light heartedness about them that Skeeter couldn't easily muster. He was 23 going on 95, it seemed. Life had no color left in it. No joy. No satisfaction. "The day I set my chickens free," he said to himself, in a kind of wishfulness that it were true in his case.

Instead of going home, he decided to go to The Doghouse, where he drank himself into a stupor. When Jack finally showed up and started his usual routine, Skeeter was dulled enough by the alcohol that it hardly seemed to register. He just nodded and smiled at him.

As Skeeter left the bar later that evening and Jack once again insisted on accompanying him out to his truck for some final words, Skeeter just kept smiling and nodding at him. But then the thought occurred to him at that moment, 'who the hell does this guy think he is, anyway? He follows me around as if we were some sort of pals, when all he really wants is to use me in place of a punching bag, to vent some of his frustration at his own shitty life.'

As he reached the truck Skeeter reached his hand behind the driver's seat and found the tire iron. As Jack approached, a nasty grin on his face, Skeeter pulled out the iron and swung it into his shin. Jack howled in pain and immediately doubled over and clutched at his throbbing leg.

Skeeter didn't stick around to see what would happen next. He slid back into the cab of the truck. The alcohol he had consumed earlier had made him a bit drowsy, but now he was wide awake and fully alert, as he slid various detritus, old empty beer cans, food wrappers, and the like, out of his way and made off before Jack could recover. He could hear Jack screaming as he drove away. "You fucking little faggot. You are dead. You hear that? You prick, you're a dead man now!"

'Oh, shit,' Skeeter's mind raced to figure out what it was he had just done, as he jammed the key in the ignition and fired up the engine and put the truck into gear, and was off and rolling down First Street.

Oops. He could see a pick up truck in the rear view mirror now, a nearly new mid 70's GMC rig with a V8 engine that he could never hope to outrun, and it was gaining on him. It had to be Jack. Fucked... Was all Skeeter could think.

The truck was now barely a car length behind him as they both barreled down Langley Road at 60 miles per hour. What to do? He suddenly swerved to the left onto Sandy Hook Road, but Jack remained right on his tail, even as he rounded the sharp turn to the right that put him onto Wilkinson Road. Now they were on a two lane straightaway for about two miles through forest and farmland, the kind of road that allowed you to really put the pedal to the floor. And Skeeter did, knowing full well that it could get you killed, as more than one drunken teen on prom night had discovered over the years. 60, 70, 80 mph. This was nuts. And Jack matched him every mile per hour. All it would take would be one deer stepping out onto the road or a car pulling out of a hidden driveway, or to lose control as the roadway veered to the left at Surface Road.

Skeeter hit the brakes as the car went into the curve and Jack tapped his bumper as he too tried to slow down. Then Skeeter made the sharp right turn onto Surface Road. This road scared him. It was a narrow asphalt strip through a dense fir forest, some of the trees so close against the asphalt roadway that their trunks lifted edges of the blacktop. The least inattention here and he could sideswipe a tree.

This stretch of roadway was unnerving for its eerie isolation as well. No one lived on this dark, gloomy stretch of road. Especially in the dark it seemed like the perfect place to meet a demented old man with one arm that ended in a hook, who carried a butcher knife that he would use to disembowel any foolish children who strayed into his domain. At least that was what he and his pals would tell each other as kids, when they would pedal all out in order to reach the safety of the main highway a mile away.

This evening Skeeter drove all out in an attempt to reach the main highway in one piece. He considered pulling over and taking his beating "like a man." After all, he had provoked this fight. But he decided that it would be better to pull over in some public area, where the presence of others might act as a bit of a social restraint on Jack.

So after he rounded the corner onto the highway heading north, he immediately pulled into the entrance of the dark grocery store on the corner of Cultus Bay Road and the highway. He didn't see anyone, but better not to continue this. Jack followed, and when Skeeter pulled to the curb, Jack was already jumping out and running toward him. The thing that startled Skeeter was the terrible rage that was written all over Jack's face as he climbed out of his truck. He wouldn't be satisfied until serious blood was shed, preferably Skeeter's and not his own, he realized. So am I going to have to really scramble just to avoid a death sentence for smacking the bastard? His mind raced for options now.

Just in the nick of time, he put the truck in reverse and, engine racing, he backed right into the grill of Jack's truck, and succeeded in bowling Jack out of the way in the process. Then he shifted into first and popped the clutch, lurching forward again and just in time to escape Jack, who was lunging for the driver side door handle. By the time he had the truck really rolling in second gear, Jack had stumbled and fallen to the pavement in the lot behind him. Then Skeeter was out the drive and on the road again, and he didn't look back as he barreled down the highway toward home.

There was no further sign of Jack as he drove on up the island toward home. He was doing fine until he hit the old back road into his place going way too fast, fueled by adrenaline and a bit fuzzy minded from too much beer. The tires failed to grip as he took a tight turn on one narrow stretch of slick, muddy road with a deep ditch on both sides. The wheels were off the road before he had time to self correct and the truck tilted dangerously close to a roll over before coming to rest against a big alder tree.

"Shit!" He swore.

Mud and slush greeted him as he crawled out the driver side window of his beat up old pick up truck. Nothing to do now but hoof it the last half mile home and come back some time after more of the snowy slush back here in the woods had melted, then retrieve the truck from the ravine where it now lay.

Who would have thought the old back road to his shack in the woods was that icy? Sure, there had been a wet snow that morning, but it had melted off the main roads and only survived in small patches back in the shaded woods. But with nightfall the temperature had dropped below freezing. Of course, if he hadn't tried to drive home at such break neck speeds after escaping mad Jack, and after an evening of sucking one too many beers at the Dog, he might have had the good sense to walk the last half mile in to his place.

And how would he get the truck out of the ditch? Fortunately, he had already hauled out the meat from the big old doe he had poached near his cabin a while back. He had gutted it and hung it in a little plywood outbuilding, and then carved it into steaks, wrapped them and hauled them out to the locker he rented from Sebering's. He had labeled the packages "lamb," so no one would be the wiser. The meat was meant to get him through another winter, when eaten with the potatoes, carrots, rutabagas and cabbage from his parent's garden, all safely tucked away in a small hand dug root cellar. Something to tide him over until he could earn a little more money, maybe working on a boat of some friend in need of crew for fishing.

Right now all he wanted was to crawl into bed and wake up in April or May. But instead he stumbled, slipping and sliding, as he made his way along the road in cold, wet shoes in the dark night. The wind whispered in the bare branches of the alders and an occasional cup of wet snow would tumble down and then drizzle down his neck and onto his bare head from out of the dark hemlock boughs. A pair of Great Horned owls were calling back and forth as they hunted the nearby forest and that eerie bark he'd heard just now might have been a fox out hunting. At least the big predators were all long gone from the island. Early settlers at Penn Cove had exterminated the wolves over a hundred years ago. The old neighbor, Charlie, down the road, said that he had seen his last cougar crossing a road way back in 1929, and the last black bear anybody claimed to have seen was in the sixties over by Lone Lake. What did the poor thing do, get tired of all the human activity and make a swim for the mainland one day?

The cabin was cold and dark, but his little black mutt of a dog was glad to be home, wagging his tail and whining in that pathetic, squeaky little voice of his. Nothing like a friend to cheer a guy up.

Robby, known among his friends as Skeeter, was a bit short on friends at the moment. A 23 year old loner from an old settler family with some Indian blood. Skagit his dad said, part of the Coast Salish people who were believed to have moved into Puget Sound some 700 years ago. Not that his Indian blood showed. He was actually a bit light in complexion with shaggy light brown hair. Stoop shouldered and wiry, of medium height and build. Not one to stand out in a crowd or a line up, which he had been in more than once.

He fired up the old wood stove, a nice old cast iron box stove with a little window to watch the flames. His Indian tv, he liked to joke. Once the fire started to heat up, he and his little Rat Dog huddled together in a chewed up old arm chair and caught the latest show and soaked up as much warmth as they could. That was a little better, he and his little pal, snug in their winter burrow, even better once he'd wrapped the wool blanket around them both.

That was just plain nuts, whacking nasty Jack with the tire iron. It wasn't the first time that an impulsive act had landed him in hot water. Alcohol and drugs seemed to increase the risk that he would do something that he might regret later. That had included rolling a car on a dark, rainy highway at four in the morning with dozing buddies along for the ride. Well, ex-buddies. Nothing like a fractured neck to sour someone on further companionship.

But this was even worse. It was one thing to accidentally injure someone, and something altogether worse to deliberately provoke a violence-prone neighbor. Like kicking a hornet's nest in this case. How did he not know that Jack had so little worth living for that he might want to kill as payback for a bruised leg. It wasn't so much the injury as the insult. He would probably spend the years in prison afterward in a state of proud acceptance of his fate, because he would take such satisfaction in what he had done to Skeeter. What do you do with a guy like that? Skeeter pulled his old single shot 20 gauge out from under the table. He would be sleeping with the shotgun by his side, for sure. No forgetting it in the truck. Fuck me, he thought as he drifted off.

Despite an overwhelming desire to just stay in bed that next day and maybe the next and the day after that, Skeeter got up and dressed and headed over to the Greenbank store on foot for some provisions. As he slowly made his way down the two track trail road back to their place, Skeeter kept his finger close to the trigger of the shot gun and the safety off. He thought maybe he would go buy himself a pistol up in Oak Harbor, something he could carry around with him, concealed. Did he have enough cash to buy a gun and buy the food and gas it would take to keep them going this winter? But could he afford not to? This thing with Jack wouldn't be over until one of them ended up injured or dead. And he knew which of them he preferred that to be.

Upon his arrival back at the cabin he discovered some further evidence of the folly of tangling with nasty Jack. There was a big hole in the window near the door. Jack had probably driven back in this morning and then snuck up just close enough to get a good shot at the window with his hunting rifle, then he had hurried away, having left his message. From the look of the hole, it was probably a 30 caliber slug that had poked the hole in the glass.

Rat Dog seemed particularly subdued. The dog rubbed against Skeeter's legs and made little whimpering sounds as he cleaned up the fragments of shattered glass on the floor near the window. His small, wiry, short haired black body seemed to tremble a bit. Lucky he had his head down when the nasty prick came through, thought Skeeter. No doubt he would have loved to take him out, if the opportunity had presented itself. No doubt there was also an exit hole somewhere in the far wall of the cabin that he would need to plug to keep the cold air out. For now he would just cover the hole with a bit of duct tape.

Chapter Six

Later that morning Skeeter used a length of cable and a hand winch to pull
the old truck out of the ditch and back onto the road. He thought at first
that he would drive back in to his place, but he couldn't bring himself to
linger in the backwoods for another minute.

His heart started pounding in his chest, as he imagined that Jack
might be driving in on his back road that very minute, and that Skeeter
might meet him head on just around the next bend in the road. He had to
get out of there.

So he set off at a reckless clip, until he remembered the bad brakes
on the old truck.He finally calmed down a bit as he reached the asphalt and
eventually made his way past the real estate office, post office and feed and
grocery store that made up downtown Greenbank. He shifted into second
to slow the old pick up truck down as he descended the big hill just north
of the Greenbank Store that led down to the loganberry farm a quarter mile
away.

Got to baby those old brake shoes as much as possible to get a
little more use out of them. He could already hear the first sounds of metal
grinding on metal when he applied the brakes, but he didn't have the
money to buy the parts for a brake job at the moment. Maybe he should
check in at the farm and see if they had any work for him.

Long rows of barren, leafless brown loganberry vines surrounded
him on both sides of the road. This was reported to be the biggest
loganberry farm in the country. The tart red berries were a cross between a
blackberry and a raspberry. Great for pies, jams and a distinctive berry
wine.

The elderly Japanese manager of Pommerelle's Loganberry Farm
had a slight smile on his face, but Skeeter didn't put much store in it, as he
asked if there was any work for him to do at the farm. He had helped
harvest the berries last summer, along with maybe a hundred other local
pickers. They had filled two gallon white plastic buckets with the juicy, tart
red berries each day for over a month and a half, beginning in early July.
The 140 acres of berries had been the source of a distinctive berry wine for
over 40 years now. It was a little on the sweet side for Skeeter's tastes, but
he sometimes bought a bottle, and he even kind of liked it on his pancakes.

The work hadn't been all that bad. He had, in fact, enjoyed being out in the field every day working with a crew of some hundred others. But one day he had gone in to the winery during a break and overheard a couple of visitors to the wine tasting room talking. "So what are we celebrating?" Asked one, and the other answered, "my new position as a lawyer for the telephone company." And his friend asked, "oh yeah, what they gonna pay you?" And the other answered, "I'll be getting $125 an hour."

When Skeeter heard this, he was totally stunned. 'Am I from another planet than these guys? How do I make $3.25 an hour for harvesting the fruit for the wine they're drinking, and those guys get $125 an hour for lawyering?' He asked himself. Somehow it just wasn't as much fun when he went back to join the others out in the field.

"I've helped out at times with the tying up of the vines. Maybe there's something else needs doing," suggested Skeeter. "I could see driving by that there are still rows where old dead vines haven't been cleared out yet and the new ones need to be gathered and tied up." Did he think that the manager didn't already know that there were still vines in need of tying up on the wire trellises? And that he was the one to do it for him?

"Sorry, not much money to pay for work right now. Bad year for sales. Owners won't let me hire more people right now. We just do the work ourselves a little at a time. Not so good, but ..." the bespectacled, elderly manager apologized to him for the lack of work.

As if he needed to apologize to Skeeter, who was the one wasting his time, when it should have been obvious that they hadn't finished that fall's fieldwork because they couldn't afford to. With the Boeing downturn and the end of the war the local economy had taken a nose dive. Gas was at an all time high. Young men who had previously been stationed overseas were flooding the job market and competition for jobs in general was fierce. And if you hadn't completed college, you weren't all that competitive to start with.

"Yeah, I understand..." Skeeter said as he climbed back into his truck.

The loganberry farm was well managed. The hardworking Japanese couple who lived in the modest farmhouse at the end of a row of seventy five year old, tall red barns had made it a model of modern agriculture. They had mechanized as much of the operation as possible and effectively employed the newest chemical tools of agribusiness. These included a substantial list of the latest pesticides, herbicides and chemical fertilizers recommended for modern American agriculture.

The manager lifted his hand to get Skeeter's attention. "I could use someone to do some spraying for me. A fungicide for the dormant winter time."

Skeeter could see that they got results, but he'd been hearing about the problems some of his buddies, returning soldiers, were having after having been sprayed with the herbicide Agent Orange over in Vietnam. So he was wary about working with the chemical sprays.

"Okay. I can work for the afternoon for you today, if you can pay me right away," he said.

Then he got busy setting up the sprayer rig on the farm tractor. The manager gave him a set of long rubber gloves, a pair of goggles and a thick rubber mask with an air filter to wear. As he drove up and down the rows applying a spray mist to the vines and soil at the base of the plants, the sun came out, and he was soon feeling overheated. The goggles were so fogged up that he could barely see where he was going. Sweat dripped down his chin from the rubber mask, and his hands were soaking wet inside the rubber gloves.

"The hell with all of this crap," he muttered, as he ripped the goggles and mask off and tossed them behind the seat. Then he slowed the tractor to a crawl as he struggled to get the sticky, wet gloves off. Once they were off, he resumed his speed. When he caught himself upwind of the spray, he would squint his eyes almost shut and take tiny breaths through his nose, as if that would prevent him from getting the spray in his eyes and lungs.

Later that afternoon, coughing and with watering eyes, he pulled the tractor back into the barn where the manager was waiting for him. He handed him a twenty dollar bill as he parked the tractor and prepared to climb down from the seat, and Skeeter muttered a "Thanks."

He felt a little dizzy as he climbed back into the truck and fumbled in his pocket for the key and then jammed it into the ignition. The truck sputtered and coughed a bit before it caught the spark and then rumbled to

life. He shifted into first and pointed it toward the entrance drive and the
300 feet of roadway that was all that comprised Wonn Road. As he turned
back onto the highway just west of the farm and started the climb up the
hill heading north, he could see little Lake Hancock in the center of the old
navy bombing range to his left and beyond that lay the Olympic Mountains
decked out in glorious white with Port Townsend's harbor and downtown
an indistinct gray mass perched at the foot of the mountains on the far
shore of Admiralty Inlet. The air was clear and bright except for the
smudge of white smoke drifting toward the mountains from the pulp mill
just east of the town.

A beautiful place for one to live and die, he mused as he sucked in
the clean, cold ocean air from the open truck window. The air felt
nourishing and sweet somehow, as if it were a lesser known but essential
member of the food pyramid. Maybe you couldn't live on it, but you
certainly couldn't live without it. But breath could be snuffed out so easily
by an oncoming car in a moment of inattention or as a result of having
pissed off the wrong person packing a gun.

But he really hated the idea of dying at the hands of a nasty, petty
prick like Jack. And so he was making the journey to Oak Harbor to buy a
gun. He had a shotgun, but he wanted a small hand gun that he could fit in
a pocket and carry everywhere he went. What other choice did he have if
he wanted to live a little longer? Fuck me, he thought. I could have avoided
this. But some perverse part of him had, on a momentary impulse, said:
"bring it on."

15 minutes later he was alongside the navy touch and go landing
field just south of Coupeville. A small gray jet plane, one of the navy's
EA6 electronic warfare aircraft, roared about fifty feet above his head.
Skeeter gaped at the underside of the jet as the dark hull swooped like an
eagle over the roadway and down to the asphalt runway beyond. "Needs a
good scrubbing," he mumbled to himself. The noise was deafening at this
proximity. 'It may be the "sound of freedom" as a sign suggested at one
exit to the base off the highway north of Oak Harbor, but if we don't make
some sort of peace with the Russians, we'll all soon be deaf around here
from the sound', he thought to himself.

Buying a gun, a little pistol, good for nothing but killing fellow
human beings. But what was the alternative? Jack had already tried to kill

him. He had to take measures to defend himself, didn't he? He could have just cringed and obeyed. Let that bastard continue to walk all over him. That's what most people did most of the time, and a lot of those who didn't do that, but chose his course of action instead, either ended up dead or in prison. But at least they hadn't backed down. A great consolation to them, I'm sure, he thought to himself as he drove.

What were the navy jets all about? Just a society trying to defend itself. And like Skeeter, the US military had taken the initiative in preemptive strikes, like he had. Fight 'em over there so we wouldn't have to fight 'em over here. So how had that worked out in Vietnam? At least the fucking Reds had learned that you don't mess with the US, hadn't they? Had they?

He cruised past Coupeville. The waterfront downtown was off to his right and the prairie farming community off to his left. As he passed the main intersection with the highway he could see the broad expanse of the prairie. The fertile green fields were created by an ancient channel of the Skagit River that deposited rich silt on the mile wide prairie. From the highway, looking west he could see the wheat, soybean and alfalfa fields with a light green fuzz from last fall's grain sowing, and beyond that he could see the frothy, shining blue waters of Admiralty Inlet and the Olympic Peninsula beyond.

And just visible on a rise at the north end of the prairie was a small log fortress built to protect the early settlers during Indian raids. White people moved onto the fertile prairie and other choice lands in the Puget Sound region with impunity in the mid nineteenth century, ignoring prior rights to this land of the local native people. So the natives had decided to make their own preemptive strike against the invaders. The rebellion had not ended well for them either. They lost nearly all of their former territories and ended up on tiny reservations, more like prisons without guards or fences. They were tossed the occasional handout to sustain life there, but they could no longer sustain their cultural ways. They no longer could practice the ancient ways of fishing and creating clothing or shelter that had sustained them for so long. It was the white man's way or no way, it seemed.

What would be Skeeter's fate for his own preemptive strike? He had cringed and obeyed for as long as he could stand it. Now he could choose to crawl off in some corner and hide, or he could perhaps risk dying at the hands of his stronger adversary. Jack represented a primitive form of the domination of the weak by the strong. And Skeeter was sick of putting up with it, and that is why he was on his way to Oak Harbor to buy a handgun now.

He arrived in Oak Harbor in late afternoon. It was an old farming community with a sizable population of conservative Christian folk of Dutch heritage. The streets of the small city's old neighborhoods were lined with big, old Garry Oaks. Their graceful sweeping branches reached out into the streets and shaded the yards in nearly a square mile of the town above the old downtown and the marina on Crescent Bay.

Skeeter discovered that the selection of pistols at the sporting goods store wasn't all that great and just about everything was out of his price range. The big naval airbase that had dominated the town since World War Two had all the real firepower. So Skeeter had to content himself with a small, cheap twenty two pistol that held a clip of five shots and might bring a rabbit down if you held it under his chin. He wouldn't be the first to discover that an improper tool made the work harder.

Jack must have been shooting at his place with some serious rifle, at least a 30 caliber, that would make a sizable hole in Skeeter if Jack could shoot straight. This peashooter would only slightly maim the victim unless the bullet struck just the right spot. A long shot, to be sure. But it, at least, gave Skeeter the illusion of fighting back.

"You call this fighting back?" he said to himself. He considered continuing north on Highway 20. He was only nine miles from the Deception Pass Bridge. Maybe it was time for him and his dog to try their luck somewhere else. They could cross the bridge and be over the mountains into eastern Washington in a few hours. He could probably find some work in an orchard.

He wouldn't be going anywhere unless he got some gas in the old truck. He waited impatiently in line at a cheap gas station. "Damn gas shortage," he grumbled. Jimmy Carter might be gaining some brownie points with the tree huggers for putting solar panels on The White House roof, but he was not so popular with the driving public. Probably the last time Americans would elect a Sunday School teacher president, he mused.

After he finally reached the pump and started filling up, he couldn't resist cursing the oil cartels as he glanced at the pump gauge and read the outrageous $1.28 a gallon on the meter. There was a soldier, looked like a marine from the Naval Air Station, filling up next to him. He was also pissed off at the price of gas.

He turned to Skeeter, as he screwed the gas cap back in place, and said, "this is too much, man, time Uncle Sam knocked a few rag heads around to get our oil back to flowing."

'Our oil?' Skeeter wondered. But then again, was it theirs, just because they ran an occasional camel over the sand dunes on top of it?

When he went in to pay his bill, he realized that he hadn't eaten anything all day. But after paying for the gas, he would be almost broke. He walked around the store looking at all of the convenience foods on the shelves, and when he thought nobody was looking, he slipped a couple of candy bars into his pocket. As he paid out the money for the gas to a friendly older woman who reminded him a bit of his mother, he felt like a real shit for ripping them off. Man, how had he sunk so low?

It took him and Rat Dog about 20 minutes to reach the rugged rock gorge that was Deception Pass. The Pass was a narrow channel about a half mile long and about two hundred yards across. The high stone walls of the gorge rose maybe 300 feet to the bridge that spanned it. And down below was a raging torrent. But as the 18th century Vancouver expedition learned, it was not the outflow of a river, but a tidal surge. The movement of the ocean tides around the island became a swift river as the water met the bottleneck of Deception Pass.

The bridge vibrated slightly under the truck and the wind created a low pitched hum as he and Rat Dog drove across the tall, narrow metal structure. Fight or flee? He asked himself as they perched on the lichen encrusted rock on the mainland side of the bridge.

From here they could see the sandy stretch of beach in the state park over on the Whidbey side and beyond that the empty horizon over the Strait of Juan de Fuca, that hundred some mile trough that ended in the broad sweep of the Pacific Ocean ending in Japan, thousands of miles distant. An eagle struck a majestic pose in a weather beaten ancient snag, a dead tree hanging precariously out over the abyss. A coal black raven called out from a tree on the cliff above and behind them, and a cold wind sent shivers down Skeeter's spine.

Fight or flee? That was the eternal question that every creature in this eat and be eaten life had to occasionally answer. And the answer always depended on a number of factors. Was the predator bigger and stronger than yourself? Was there a reasonable path for escape, if it came to that? Was there another way out, maybe appear larger and more threatening than you were, or roll over and play dead, or at least feign subservience?

Jack was not your average predator. He was willing to go for broke, if he thought that the occasion required it. He remembered one time at a Holmes Harbor Gun Cub event, Jack had grabbed an ex-girl friend roughly by the wrist and shouted at her: "Don't you ignore me, bitch!" Everyone in the room turned toward the two of them. Then Jack struck a threatening pose and shouted at them all: "Come on, I'm ready to go to hell if you are!"

Nobody took him up on the offer and after a few minutes the hapless girl quietly and submissively left the gathering with Jack on her arm. What do you do with a guy like that? Some day he might go too far and land himself in prison after crippling or killing one of his victims, but until then he would probably terrorize a whole community. Skeeter, however, didn't feel much like becoming a hero or a martyr to the cause of ridding the community of this menace.

But there he was, sitting on this rock, at a place that should have filled his soul with delight, surrounded by the raw, wild beauty of this northern outlet to the Pacific Ocean. A place that could easily remind one of the triviality and unimportance of most human activity in the greater scheme of things. Our simian species was really just a small blip in the greater fossil record of life forms on the earth. We had skulked around the fringes for a couple hundred thousand years and then rose to a position of dominance in just the past couple thousand years, and we had really outdone ourselves in the past hundred. It was an impressive, rather meteoric rise, and one that seemed like it could as easily end soon in a meteoric crash, if we weren't careful. And Skeeter had a suspicion that we weren't, and probably never would be a careful species, except in isolated cases. But, then again, we're talking about a pretty clever and adaptable monkey much of the time.

Interesting speculation, but not very helpful in resolving his immediate dilemma. A guy he met by the bridge told him that he should forget about crossing the mountains on Highway 20. The pass was closed. Too much snow this year. Might not open for another month. After a time, he seemed to have made up his mind. He called Rat Dog, who was sniffing around the foliage in the near vicinity. They got back into the truck and Skeeter turned the truck around and headed back onto the island.

Chapter Seven

As darkness approached Skeeter drove back in to his cabin exhausted. But
after only a few minutes there he grew so anxious that he couldn't sit still.
Then, as quickly as possible he began loading up everything he thought he
might need. This included some of his clothes and bedding, a few pots and
pans and his shotgun and a wreck of an old 30 caliber Japanese World War
Two bolt action carbine rifle that his dad had brought back from the war.
Skeeter had forgotten that he even had the old relic, but recent events had
stirred his memory, and he was reaching for any and all possible weapons
he might employ in his "war" with Jack. He also found a six inch buck
knife in a drawer to add to his arsenal. Rat Dog, Rat Dog's bedding and a
half bag of cheap dog food completed the inventory of items to take with
him.

He drove with no clear idea of where they were going. He just
knew that they had to get out of there. It was about eight in the evening
when he found himself somewhere near the downtown in Seattle. Skeeter
exited the freeway at Mercer Street and pulled the truck down a side street
in what looked like an industrial district of the city. There should be some
places here where he could park for the night without getting hassled by
the cops.

They found a spot on a street lined by what looked like small
manufacturing shops. The buildings were aging, dark brick and cinder
block things with tall, dirty windows on second floors and with
windowless warehouse doors leading up to loading docks on the street
level. The work day was over and there were only a few dim lights on the
street and several parked cars and no people.

He fumbled around for the pistol, and then got out, leaving Rat
Dog locked in the truck, whining. The dark city street, devoid of people,
made him nervous. He needed to find something to eat, so he headed
toward a street that seemed to be a major thoroughfare, brighter and noisy
with the sounds of traffic.

Once he had arrived there he almost immediately noticed the sign
for a tavern further up the street. That would have to do. So he hiked up the
street and went into the dimly lit bar. There was a friendly enough looking
crowd. It appeared to be a neighborhood bar where a modest looking

assortment of working people and low income retired folk gathered in the evening.

It didn't feel all that strange to him. There were even a couple of younger guys who looked like they could be vets. No one really stared at him. They seemed to accept the arrival of strangers among them without much curiosity or concern.

He took a place at the bar and ordered a beer and a hamburger with fries. There was a song playing on a juke box in one corner. Some dated fifties love song, the final words drifting his way: "your chances are, awfully good."

'Chances of what?' He asked himself. Getting mugged down here. One of the younger guys approached the bar to order another beer. He looked Skeeter over a bit on the sly, then said, "How you doin', man. I ain't seen you around before. You new around here?"

"Yeah," Skeeter replied. "Just came into town this evening. Me and my dog are camped out in my truck on a side street."

"That should be cool. You'll see that there are a few other people camping in cars around here. I got a little hole in the wall place in a wreck of a building. In the morning you can go down the street to the Lutheran Church for some coffee. The community center behind the church has a food bank and a soup kitchen going too. Folks are pretty cool."

"Thanks, man. I'll probably need to check them out tomorrow."

After his burger and beer and a visit to the toilet, he returned to the truck. He let Rat Dog out to do his thing in the bushes. Then he got out a couple bowls for some food and water for the dog. The street remained dark and quiet as the dog ate his supper and Skeeter looked on. A block over he could see a little activity around a parked car. It appeared to be someone else living out of a car. It looked to be an older couple. They were unrolling some bedding in the back of an old station wagon. It was a sign to him that this was a rather benign neighborhood for the down and out to bed down in. He started preparing something similar in the truck cab for him and the dog.

The next morning, after a restless night that seemed like it would never end, he climbed out of the truck and stretched stiff, aching limbs. The dog hurried off to the same blackberry thicket he had visited the night before. Then he found a length of old rope and tied it around Rat Dog's neck and led him down the street toward the church. Rat Dog had only been on a rope a couple times in his life, and he kept wanting to go off and investigate things, only to be tugged back onto the straight and narrow of the sidewalk.

The side door to the church was open and he could see a short line formed up in front of a big aluminum coffee urn. A number of down and outers, not too unlike Skeeter himself, men of various ages, unkempt looking, obviously sleeping in the rough somewhere, stood passively waiting their turn. Skeeter tied Rat Dog to a nearby lamp pole and got in line, and when his turn came he filled the styrofoam cup and added a little powdered coffeemate. Then he retrieved Rat Dog and the two of them sat down on a little patch of grass near the church building and Skeeter rolled himself a smoke.

"Hey, man, could you spare one of those?" He heard a raspy voice ask. He looked up to see a young guy with long, dirty brown hair in a green army fatigue jacket, standing over them, holding his own styrofoam cup of coffee.

"Sure, man. Here you go." And Skeeter handed him a cigarette paper and the bag of tobacco. Then he pulled out a book of matches and handed those to him as well.

"Thanks, man. I really appreciate that."

After he had rolled his cigarette and lit it, the two of them just sat there and drank their coffee and smoked their cigarettes in silence. Then they spied a couple of men in expensive suits, carrying leather brief cases, coming their way down the sidewalk. His new pal asked the men, "could you spare a little change, man?"

They looked at Skeeter and his new friend as if they were looking at cockroaches or some other mildly repulsive creature. Then one of them reached into his briefcase, giving the panhandler some momentary sense of hope that he might have scored this time. But when the man withdrew his hand, he had a book in it.

"Oh, no,' thought Skeeter. 'Is it gonna be a Bible?' But what he thrust into his pal's hand was a different book.

"Read this, and you'll understand why I can't give you any money," and he gave his friend a mischievous grin as he handed the book to the beggar. Then the two of them hurried off down the street.

Skeeter and his pal studied the cover: *The Fountainhead* by Ayn Rand. His pal tossed the book down in disgust and walked off. Skeeter picked up the book and started reading some of it. He liked the story. Kind of a gripping story of suffering followed by redemption, when the hero, an architect, gets to build a grand skyscraper. All of it funded by a cruel, ruthless rich patron. Great story. But it only made him feel worse about himself. Too bad people like him were such losers. Not like the creative, resourceful hardworking architect in this story. If Ayn Rand was right, then guys like him and his new pal should just go off in some corner and die, and save the world the trouble of killing them.

He spent the rest of that morning getting himself clued into a whole community of the homeless, the near homeless and the network that allowed them to survive, if not thrive in this odd little neighborhood, tucked away amidst warehouses and shops just off the freeway on the edge of the downtown.

He visited the community center set up in an old house behind the church later that morning. It seemed to be run by a strange bunch of idealistic young people. There was a walk in medical clinic, a food bank, a clothing bank, and a kitchen with a dining area. There was information on emergency and social services and a mix of leftist political pamphlets, books and newspapers. Local artists had painted murals on the walls depicting a world of trees and flowers and animals and people living a tad bit better and more harmoniously than those who mingled in the dining area.

Yet, there seemed to be more cheer and hope here than seemed warranted by the reality. There were the haunted looking old and young guys. Ragged looking, gaunt, unshaven guys who probably had a hard luck story not too different from Skeeter's own. But there were others as well. Poor folk who lived in the run down old houses and apartments hidden among the tool shops and warehouses. They seemed to be trying to make the best of the fact that their neighborhood, a century or more old, had gone to seed. They walked their dogs in the little park across the street and chatted with one another over lunch in the center. The staff of the center seemed oblivious to much of the squalor that surrounded them. They just went about their business, problem solving the delivery of supplies, the preparation of food, and the maintenance of the facilities. They interacted cheerfully enough with the neighborhood, the poor and often lonely elderly, the struggling single mothers, the crippled, the mentally unbalanced and the down and out strangers who found their way to their door.

If someone like Skeeter asked them a question, they were quite willing to temporarily drop whatever they were doing and give him some of their attention. This wasn't some well-funded government agency staffed by bureaucrats. It was a ragtag operation funded by some neighborhood grant program that paid some local people a minimum wage to operate the center.

Although material resources were quite limited at the center, the staff gladly shared what they had. If there was a slight air of tension, it came from the occasional lost soul who wandered in, but even the most deranged visitor tended to treat the people and the facilities of the center with the respect such a haven from despair deserved.

Skeeter and Rat Dog found a niche there. So they stayed on in the neighborhood, just biding their time. Skeeter even found a couple of days work in a warehouse through a temp agency. He helped repair some damaged roofing on the center building, and he and Rat Dog even enjoyed little parties in the park or on the stoops of the buildings, or an evening in the center, when someone might play a guitar and someone else might share a six pack of beer, and there would be singing and stories shared into the evening. Even the people like Skeeter, who had little to say, and precious little to share, were welcome among them. The nights, as usual, were the worst for him. He clutched his dog and his gun in the dark truck cab. Startled awake repeatedly by a truck backfiring on the freeway or the crash of a broken bottle on a nearby street corner, and never without a bad dream or two, his nights were an ordeal.

One morning about a week after his arrival there, he let Rat Dog out of the truck as usual to do his thing, and the little dog failed to return, as usual, after a couple minutes. He called him. "Hey, guy, where have you gotten to? Come on, time for breakfast!"

But still no dog. Now he was getting a little worried. Where the hell was the little mutt? This was no place to go wandering off on your own. "Hey, dog!" He shouted. And then he heard a faint whine, off in some bushes in a vacant lot just off the freeway ramp. It was a favorite place for some of the homeless to bed down in cardboard shelters or under plastic sheets or the occasional ragged little tent.

He cautiously pushed his way in to the bushes. You never knew what might be back in there. That's when he saw the dog, sitting and staring at something on the ground in front of him. Skeeter didn't want to get any closer, but he wanted to get the dog out of there, so he pushed his way further into the bramble thicket, oblivious to the sharp thorns.

The old man. What? Thirty nine, maybe? Was lying on his side. He was still wrapped in the ragged, dirty old overcoat that he had used to try and stay warm. Had he frozen to death? Maybe had a heart attack. No signs of foul play. But he was definitely dead. There was something about a corpse. None of the life force and animation of even a sleeping body. And, well, there were the flies too, that were beginning to hover over him. A dead giveaway. Ha ha. Bad joke.

He grabbed Rat Dog by the scruff of his neck and tried to pull him away. The dog resisted. He couldn't seem to take his eyes off the man. Neither could Skeeter. But he wanted to be away from there as quickly as possible. And he wanted his dog away from there too.

Reluctantly the dog finally quit resisting him, and the two of them returned to the truck and Skeeter drove to the next block over and parked. He fed Rat Dog, and they headed over to the church and got in line for some coffee. Skeeter kept wondering if he should report what he'd found? But he didn't want to get involved. Police questioning and all that. So he just hoped it wouldn't be too long before someone else found the dead bum. Yeah, that's all he was. A dead bum. Someone that nobody was going to miss or mourn his passing. Just suck it up, man. It was that guy's turn. You're still a ways back in line, so to speak. No reason to take it personally, he said to himself.

Later that day, with nothing better to do, he and Rat Dog roamed the nearby downtown Pike Place Market. As they were passing the bookstore full of radical political stuff, he glanced over at the books displayed in the window and decided, what the hell, and went in to browse around. It wasn't long before he was surrounded by books that he'd pulled off the shelves to study, and Rat Dog lay contentedly sprawled out on the floor, napping.

No one paid him any special mind, or seemed to care. So it wasn't long before he was coming into the store once or twice a day, reading books and newspapers as if he were in a public library. It was an excuse to get in off the street, into a warm, dry space for a while, but there were other places where he could do that. The community center, and, of course, public libraries, and there were coffee shops, but then he would have to at least buy a cup of coffee, and Rat Dog wasn't welcome in that many places, either. It wasn't long before he was a familiar face to the staff, and they began to interact with him, say hello, recommend books, pet Rat Dog, and the like.

It was, maybe, Skeeter's fourth visit to the market and the bookstore that things got more interesting. He said hello to the woman at the front desk, Joanne, whom he had met on an earlier visit to the store. Then he asked her if Peter, the German Jewish head of the collective that ran the store, was around. She told him that Peter was in back somewhere, finishing tallying up yesterday's receipts. Then a grey haired, bespectacled older man, who looked more like he still belonged in some university department than running an anarchist bookstore that catered to those hell bent on revolution, stuck his head out of the back room and said, "I'll be through here soon."

Skeeter waited up front in the store with the dowdy, middle aged, bespectacled woman, who volunteered in the bookstore. She studied Skeeter for a few moments, and then spoke to him in a near whisper, so that Peter wouldn't be likely to overhear her.

"You know he's crazy, don't you? He's on medication to deal with it. He left the university on mental disability."

So she wanted to warn him off involvement with Peter. But Skeeter hardly acknowledged her words. Just a slight nod of the head. It hadn't taken Skeeter very long, when listening to Peter's impassioned talk about the corrupt, decadent American military, economic and political system, to gather that he had long ago abandoned the dispassionate discourse of a university professor.

Then he proceeded on into the back of the store to where Peter was working. He looked up from his counting, and when he saw Skeeter, he said, "I wondered if I had scared you off or made you more curious. How is your reading going?"

"Fine," he replied, as he gazed around him at the rows of colorful covers of the paperback books that lined the shelves. The store was rather small, but held a surprising collection of books that ranged from fine poetry and fiction to tomes on philosophy and anthropology, and, of course, a large section on communist and anarchist political thought, most of it classic European, which meant Karl Marx himself, some more recent political philosophers, and the works of Russian anarchists such as Bakunin and Kropotkin, and the Russian American transplants, Emma Goldman and Alexander Berkman. He felt like there was a world of radical thinking to explain this fucked up world, to keep him busy reading for years to come. And Peter usually had a new book to thrust into his hands, with the words, "Here, you need to read this."

And today, as usual, he pointed out several books that he thought that Skeeter would like. He, in fact, usually did find whatever book was recommended by the slightly seedy looking, old professor interesting.

"Let's go across the street to the Soup and Salad Restaurant for some coffee," suggested Peter.

Skeeter followed him across the cobbled market street out front of the store and into a three story building that, on the street level, had dozens of vendor stalls where seafood, produce and craft vendors and a restaurant or two served the hundreds of market goers who came to the downtown market every day. They hiked up a set of stairs and ducked into the enclosed second story of the building, where more small shops with a wide variety of wares from comic books to clay pots greeted shoppers. After a few twists and turns down the steep hallway they arrived at the entrance to the cooperative, worker-owned restaurant.

A tall, slim, pretty girl met them at the cash register, where she poured coffee into thick, white clay mugs for them from a stainless steel pot. After stirring the usual cream and sugar into the translucent brown brew, they took seats next to each other at a counter facing a broad window that looked out on Elliott Bay. A large ferryboat had just left the dock to the south of them on its hourly trip over to Winslow over on Bainbridge Island. The far shore over on the Peninsula side of the Sound was only faintly visible. Seagulls floated past the window and pigeons lined a ledge on a building just across the way and slightly below their seats.

Peter stroked his short, gray beard thoughtfully as he gazed out on the bay. Skeeter had already heard some of the story of Peter's boyhood. How he had grown up in an educated Jewish household in Vienna, among the elite of the city's intelligentsia, mingling with Central Europe's scientific and cultural elite. He had witnessed the pitched battle between the socialist government and their rivals in the city in the 1930's, and the Nazi victory in 1938 that led to his parents packing him off to an American university at the age of 17. He had gone on to a career as a university professor in physics. He had even taken his family to Israel in the 1950's in hopes that the new state would match his high ideals, which it did not. When the political activism of the 1960's reinvigorated the radical American left wing movement, Peter left academia and jumped into the fray with strongly held anarcho-communist beliefs forged over a lifetime.

Peter, with his strong German accent and intellectual sophistication, would have seemed an odd match with Skeeter, the young army veteran with his rather simple country ways. Yet, they had found common ground and had developed a surprisingly easy rapport.

Peter's deep, sonorous voice had a rather gentle teacher's tone as he discussed American history and current politics with Skeeter. "Seattle has had its popular rebellions against the ruling class. The Seattle general strike of 1919 was like nothing before it in American history. The workers took control of the city and showed how unnecessary the ruling class really was. That sort of thing was not so uncommon in Europe. The Paris Commune, for instance, in the mid 19th century had shown the world the growing power of the common people united."

There was so much that Skeeter knew so little about. He felt like such an ignorant redneck in comparison with someone like Peter. But he was impressed by the fact that Peter didn't make him feel like a stupid fool, just someone who was only now being exposed to ideas and knowledge and history that had eluded him in the past. The only requirement for Skeeter to gain Peter's respect was to show a capacity for genuine curiosity about the world around him.

"I really liked Howard Zinn's *Peoples' History of the United States*. I think that his American history is pretty spot on. It helps explain a lot of the meanness and stupidity I see around me," Skeeter told him.

"No doubt, what he has to say about the military's role in extending American power and influence far beyond our borders must have struck some chord with you."

Skeeter nodded his assent. Despite the rather thick German accent, there was something engaging about Peter's speech. He spoke with a certain elegance and articulation that was new to Skeeter. Most of the people in Skeeter's world spoke only about practical matters in simple, almost blunt speech. The two of them must have sat there for over an hour, discussing a wide range of topics. Skeeter was like a sponge soaking up every bit of knowledge Peter shared with him.

As they were about to leave, an ancient, weathered old man in a ragged old wool coat and a gray wool cap with long ear flaps came in the door. He poured himself a cup of coffee and hobbled over to the table next to them. When he saw Peter he gave him a slight nod in recognition, and then turned his scowling face to the challenge of lifting the cup of coffee to his lips with a trembling hand without spilling any of the contents.

Peter smiled at the man and said, "Hi, Joe, how have you been?"

The old man looked over at Peter through rheumy eyes and in a gravelly voice, muttered, "The Bulls, those damn sons of bitches, took my revolver from me yesterday. How am I supposed to protect myself from the young punks out there on the streets without my gun? Can you try and get it back for me?"

"I can ask. But did you threaten anybody with it?" He asked.

"Well, hell yes, of course, what's the point of carrying a gun if people don't know that you have it and you're willing to use it?" He growled. "The Everett Massacre would have never happened if we'd been really armed."

Peter smiled at this, and he turned to Skeeter and asked, "Do you know about the Everett Massacre?"

Skeeter shook his head no.

"It happened back in November of 1916 in the town of Everett. Joe here was a young millworker back then, weren't you, and a member of the union, the Industrial Workers of the World, known as the Wobblies?"

"You're damned right I was," growled Joe. "You think the bosses are bad today. Back then a working stiff put in a ten hour day, and the boss payed you whatever he damn well pleased and could boot your ass out if you looked at him crossed eyed. You're damned right, we organized and we fought back."

"So were you one of the workers in Everett who tried to organize a union and the company thugs beat up?" Asked Peter.

"Hell no. But I was on the boat, the Verona, that the union hired to take a group of us from Seattle to Everett to support the organizers there. We were all madder than hell after hearing the story about how the company thugs had made our union boys up there run a gauntlet where they beat the hell out of them. We heard they even beat our men with devil's club stalks." He looked as angry as if it had happened yesterday.

"You can bet we were plenty mad and the Bulls knew it," he continued, with a fierce scowl. "I don't think they wanted to arrest us. Last time they did that we tore the hell out of the jail. So this time, when we reached Everett they were there waiting at the dock as we got off the boat. They claimed that one of our boys fired on them, but I don't believe it. Sure, somebody maybe did. There was a guy or two with some little peashooter on him. But those cops and hired thugs and even members of the local American Legion, who met us, were armed to the teeth. They just gunned our men down. It was a massacre alright, a couple of them died and about a dozen of our boys, and then they blamed us. Put some 75 of us on trial and none of them. That's American justice for you." And he shook his head in disgust.

"But the jury did let those men off and your movement went on to secure our right to free speech and to organize, and that led in the 1930's to things like the minimum wage, the 40 hour work week, workmen's compensation, and an end to child labor," Peter listed the movement's accomplishments on his fingers.

"So what? These punk kids today don't have a clue about how we had to fight and suffer to get those rights. And you can bet they won't keep them either, if they aren't prepared to organize and fight for their rights." And he glowered at Skeeter as he said this.

"Those who fail to learn from history are doomed to repeat it," said Peter, repeating a famous old phrase from a philosopher.

But there was more to Peter than just bookish knowledge. There was a gleam to his eyes as he spoke. He passionately wanted this world to be transformed, and his readings of history told him that this could only happen in a painful and bloody birth of the new society where freedom, justice and equality would flourish.

Skeeter easily picked up on this from their talks, but it didn't scare him off. He felt like he had nothing to lose. In his own way, he was as eager to break out of the invisible chains that held him as Peter was. What was it the violent revolutionaries of Europe had proclaimed: "You have nothing to lose but your chains." Yes, he could easily get behind that way of thinking.

Peter, no doubt sensed this as well, as he turned and spoke to him in a hushed voice. "I have some people that I want you to meet. Can you join us after I finish a few things at the store, at a tavern over in the U. District?"

"Yeah, sure," answered Skeeter, as they made their way back to the store.

Once they had entered the bookstore, Peter said, "Oh, and while I finish up here, why don't you read some of this material we have on the veteran's movement." And he handed Skeeter a couple of books and pamphlets to study while he waited.

There was so much to learn. So much political and social history seemed deliberately buried away in obscure, odd little book shops or rare book collections in some graduate research library somewhere. Guys like him normally had little or no access to this kind of thing. He had always been told that we were "the arsenal of democracy" and champions of peace and freedom. Now here were some very persuasive people telling him otherwise. He read a line that declared: "Our armed forces are often employed to overthrow governments of foreign lands who interfere in the profitable overseas enterprises of American corporations such as United Fruit and Standard Oil."

Then he read further down: "Our government was among the key organizers of the International Criminal Court to try international war criminals, and we were among the sponsors of the United Nations and its universal declaration of human rights. But our government refuses to abide by the decisions of that court or the principles of the declaration. It is called American exceptionalism, but it is nothing more nor less than American imperialism."

It had sounded so strange to him to hear somebody call his country imperialist. But we were the dominant power in the world, and as such, no one had been able to force us to abide by the rules that we had helped forge for others to live by. He read on: "We like to call other nations that don't abide by those rules rogue states."

But he knew from experience that if you dared call America that, you were called a communist or worse, and guys like Jack would be glad to beat the shit out of you for it. All of this new information that he was taking in was fueling his anger. Skeeter could feel it rising in him like a volcano that was ready to explode any time now. Somebody had to pay for the shit out there. He felt hot all of the sudden. He was nervous and edgy. He waited impatiently for Peter to finish his work. He tossed all the papers aside in disgust and went outside and rolled himself a cigarette. He wanted to do something...

After Peter had finished his work, they set off in their separate cars for the U. District. They met back up at a cozy tavern called The Roost, just south of the University Bridge. There were some college age guys, with long, flowing manes, and an occasional mustache, chatting at the bar, and a group of oddly clean cut, slightly older people over at a table in one dimly lit corner of the room, who waved to Peter as they entered. Peter led him over to the table in the corner, where he introduced Skeeter to the group, and they ordered some beer and sat down with them. For some odd reason one of them was telling about the gory details of how a transsexual's sex organs were surgically altered.

"First they make an incision that runs from..." a clean cut guy, who looked sort of like a frat boy, droned on through an increasingly thick smoke haze and a beer buzz, that matched the increasing buzz in the room as more customers filed in. Why was this guy talking about this with a sort of demented gleam in his eye? Peter had suggested that he was going to meet some movement heavies, serious people who wanted to do some serious shit. Which this wasn't. After a time, though not soon enough for Skeeter's liking, Peter slipped him a piece of paper with a contact phone number on it. Apparently to a public pay phone, one among many that they used. Then they said that they would be in touch and the group broke up and headed to their cars.

On the way home Skeeter thought, 'Who are these people? Why did Peter take me to some bar to meet people who just talked about silly shit? Maybe they just wanted to check me out before inviting me in to anything more serious? That might make sense. It sure was odd though. Then again this whole city crowd were an odd bunch as far as he could tell. Was it the result of people all living so crowded together, nearly on top of one another? Most of them in little boxes stacked up five and even ten high in apartment buildings?'

'From the way Peter talked,' mused Skeeter, 'I thought I was going to meet our local version of the SLA, the San Francisco based group of armed militants who had lashed out at the whole, ugly machine a while back, and made some dents in it before they died in a fiery blaze of glory.' Skeeter kind of liked the idea of that, when the alternative seemed to be dreary resignation to a life of abuse and exploitation by those with all the power. Better a quick and honorable death after making the master class pay a bit for their crimes. How he would love to lay a pipe bomb in the fat lap of some manufacturer of land mines, or put a bullet into the finely coiffed head of a corporation that makes napalm. But those were just crazy thoughts, the kind that would sometimes just enter his head, from who knows where.

The next morning, while walking a nearby street, Skeeter noticed a set of small garage-like structures all in a row, newly built from the look of them. One of the garage doors was open and he could see a collection of furniture, some chairs and a table, a sofa, and lamps, and even a set of dishes. The space had several lights and he could see a heater unit in one wall. A local homeless guy, with his gear in a small shopping basket, was passing by about then, and Skeeter turned to him and said, "kind of looks like a shelter for homeless folk. Is that what it is?"

"Nah," said the guy. "Nothin' like that. They're buildin' storage places nowadays for people to put all their extra shit. What they can't use, and don't have no place to store at home."

"Oh," said Skeeter. "Yeah, I guess so..."

Chapter Eight

One day, not long after, there was a flurry of activity at the community
center when word came that the cops were on their way to evict a whole
building of low income tenants in a nearby building. He followed the
crowd over to the building entrance and stood there watching as staff from
the center tried to block the eviction with their bodies. They were easily
enough handcuffed and tossed into the backs of waiting patrol cars. As
usual, the demands of wealthy landlords trumped the needs of
impoverished tenants.

     Although Skeeter watched in growing anger, he didn't see the point
of getting arrested along with the others. There were a number of guys like
him in the crowd looking on at the spectacle unfolding in front of them. He
could see his own anger reflected in their eyes. They had built the
buildings and fought the wars for the owners, but when they were no
longer useful to them, they were cast out to fend for themselves. Trash to
be cleared out at the owners' whim.

     Would they fight back? Probably not, against the authorities.
Military life had taught most of them some hard lessons about bucking
authority. No. They would passively watch as these wimpy, idealistic
college kids got their asses hauled off to jail for defying the powers that be.
And he kept reminding himself that he didn't have a dog in this fight. And
anyway, what did they hope to accomplish. Somebody said something
about "making a statement." It was a pathetic statement, as far as he could
tell.

     But he suddenly felt ashamed as he saw someone he knew from
the bookstore collective join those blocking the entrance and getting
arrested. New people kept stepping forward and getting arrested, one after
another. As Joanne, elderly and overweight, stood there with the others,
she looked Skeeter over carefully, rather surprised at how he seemed to
have sunk in the world. He could tell that she pitied him. One more lost
vet, roaming the streets with no good purpose or plan to his life. It was
almost unbearable to see himself in the eyes of this other. He resolved at
that moment to do something about it.

He arrived at the bookstore around closing time again. This time a cheerful woman about his age was tallying sales on a little hand held computer. She had met Skeeter in the store earlier that month, and she knew that Peter had formed a friendship of sorts with him. She looked up from her work and smiled at him. "Hi, how are you doing?"

That question always left him with mixed feelings. Did anybody really want to hear him whine about things? Probably not. "Okay. Is Peter around?"

"No, he is over at his little houseboat on Portage Bay by the U." She answered without looking up from her work.

"Oh, would it be okay if I go over there to find him?" He asked.

This time she paused and looked up from her work, studying his face briefly before answering.

"Sure, here, let me draw you a quick map." And she proceeded to draw a map for him, and then handed it to him and returned to her work.

"Thanks," he said, as he headed back out the door, into a chill, damp evening. The cobblestone on the street at the corner of Pike and First glistened in the newly lit street lamp light. An Indian stood at the corner, just staring about him in dazed silence, as if he had gone to bed the night before in a quiet, little native fishing village on the shores of the Salish Sea, and awoke the next morning to this nightmare of concrete and cars and crazy white people as far as the eye could see. Pike Place Market shoppers were making their final purchases of the day, and even the street people, the winos and the mentally unbalanced, who haunted this part of town, were also retreating to warmer regions of the public space.

All of the sudden the Indian began shouting: "You white people are all crazy. You're all gonna die when Mother Earth decides to shake you off her back like so many fleas. And then the big water is gonna come and wash you all out into the ocean. You and your big cars and fancy houses!"

'Boy, what a nut case,' thought Skeeter, as he fumbled for his keys in the dim light and eventually got the door opened, much to the relief of Rat Dog, who leapt out and rushed over to a nearby lamp post and peed. Then they drove through the wet streets of downtown. Lights were coming on in the three to four story buildings that surrounded them, and he could see the twenty some story Smith Tower to the south, Seattle's tallest building, beginning to glow as tenants who hadn't quite finished their day's work turned on more lights.

He eventually found the little houseboat on Portage Bay, looking out across the water at the University of Washington. It was already dark and the lights across the way cast flickering reflections on the churning surface of the bay. There was one dim, yellow light showing through the cloth curtain on the stern end window of the boat.

He and Rat Dog approached the boat cautiously, but the boat shifted slightly as he quietly stepped aboard and rapped lightly on the door. Peter drew the curtain aside and peered out into the dark momentarily and then opened the door to him. "Skeeter," he said and smiled as he quickly led him over to a small table.

"I'm here, and I'm in a bit of trouble back home," he muttered, not looking at Peter, but down at the floor, where Rat Dog sat, looking up adoringly at his human pal. It was obvious that he had been sleeping in the rough. His hair was long and shaggy and his usually trim beard had grown wooly. His clothes didn't look much better. His blue jeans and flannel shirt were rumpled and gave off a slightly mildewed smell. His eyes were puffy and had dark rings around them.

Peter looked at him with what appeared to be genuine concern. "Sit down," and he gestured for him to take a chair next to him in the cramped, little kitchen area of the boat. "I have some cheese and bread from the market, and some red wine."

They ate for a while in silence. Skeeter tossed Rat Dog an occasional scrap of bread that seemed to satisfy him. Then Skeeter said, "I fucked up. There's a guy who has been making my life miserable since I was a little kid out on the island, and I just snapped one night and gave him a taste of what he's been handing me for years. If I stay on the island one of us is probably going to die. I don't know why I did what I did."

"I do," said Peter. "You'd had enough. I know what it's like to suffer such humiliation at the hands of thugs. When the Nazis started to get the upper hand in Vienna back in the 1930's, we Jewish kids, as well as the adults, were special targets of their abuse. We should have fought harder when we had the chance back then. But in the end we just cringed and obeyed, biding our time, thinking that this would pass. Their movement would fizzle out eventually, built as it was on false promises. If only we had known what was really in store for us…" And he shook his head at the sad memory.

"I know first hand what most Americans don't have a clue about. That you can't let yourself be intimidated by the fascist thugs around you. You have to fight back. It is better to take the battle to the enemy. You have to strike before they have a chance to." And he slammed his fist down on the table to dramatize his point.

Skeeter had never seen this side of Peter. It shocked him a bit, but it wasn't because it was strange to him. No, it was actually all too familiar.

"I know the place we can put you up in, and the people there would benefit from some of your experience." Peter said all of this with gleaming eyes that seemed to penetrate Skeeter, looking into his innermost being.

What did that look mean? Skeeter wondered, from this grizzled, white haired old professor in front of him, whose family had been driven out of Nazi Central Europe in 1938, forcing him to pursue university in America. He and his parents had had to watch from afar in horror as the monsters destroyed their family and friends along with nearly the entire European Jewish society. And Skeeter, what did Peter see when he looked at him? A bitterly disillusioned young man, feeling utterly betrayed by those in leadership in America. Men who should have recognized that their land war in Southeast Asia was a colossal blunder after only the first years, but who, out of pride, ignorance and I suppose just plain denial of the facts in front of them, let the death and destruction drag on for years.

No doubt, both he and Peter spent a good deal of their time brooding over the injury and injustice of the world that had not spared them personally. More than anything else, Peter wanted to strike out at those he held most responsible for the misery in his life. He had honed in on those in power, the privileged, pampered ruling class. And he had pretty much convinced Skeeter that his prime enemy was the American military industrial political complex. Just let them commit an act or two of vengeance on their rulers before their police finally brought them down. But let them get some payback first. He did want peace, of sorts, but if any such thing were really possible, it seemed to Skeeter that it would probably only come with death or during life imprisonment.

Peter led him on a footpath that followed the contour of the bay until they were maybe a mile up from the houseboat. Then he guided him up some stairs to a small apartment building that stood a block up from the water and indicated that he should buzz one of the ground floor apartments. "There is a safe house here that we rented a while back. You will need to park your truck at a distance and approach the house from the foot trail along the water where you can spot anyone who might be following you. Our comrades in a cell of the GJB, like those you met the other night, will be there."

GJB, the George Jackson Brigade, the notorious local political gang who were responsible for bombings and robberies all over the Puget Sound, and who were hunted by some of America's top agents of the FBI. Were they really so hard to find? Here Skeeter was, recruited into their circle after only a few visits with Peter at the store. Why was it so easy for him to be accepted, while the government had such trouble locating and identifying members of the group? And Peter was such an obvious link to the group. Or was Skeeter so accepted? Maybe this would be when he would find out how much they did or did not trust him.

After retrieving his truck, he once again approached the slightly seedy looking two story brick building that probably catered to a student population. He studied the series of metal mailboxes at the entrance. They were a bit beat up and grimy looking and the paper name labels were old and tattered, so he had to search a bit to find the party he was looking for. He pushed the buzzer for the apartment with no idea whether it sounded in the apartment. But seconds later an unpleasantly loud and grating buzzing sound at the entrance door told him that he was being ushered in.

Here goes, he thought to himself. Am I really ready for this? A little late for such thoughts, but the thought wasn't to be denied. He really had no good idea of who these people were, but here he was, going into their safe house.

The door opened a crack and the muzzle of a pistol appeared, pointed at his chest. Skeeter winced and drew back slightly. Then found his voice. "Peter sent me."

The door then opened more widely and a slim woman with short black hair motioned him in with the hand that held the .44 magnum revolver. "Who the fuck are you?" she snarled. Then a clean cut, preppy looking guy that he had met at the bar with Peter, emerged from the adjoining room and said, "It's Peter's friend. Hey, you came to join up, eh?"

There was a group of five of them, sitting around the table, drinking cheap red wine and talking about "targets." "We've got to show them that the capture of John and Ed in that botched bank robbery won't even slow the struggle down." He was referring to John Sherman and Ed Meade, members of the George Jackson Brigade, who had been arrested a while back at a Tukwila bank, when their timing of an armed robbery proved incredibly bad. A police car arrived within minutes of the bank robbers.

"Let's shut the fucking lights off! Blow up a power transformer. A central one, supplying power to the downtown," came a suggestion.

"Yeah, that sounds good. You got any experience with explosives, man?" Someone asked Skeeter.

"A little," he muttered. 'Who the hell are these jerks?' He asked himself. What could blowing up a transformer achieve except to piss off a lot of people, maybe even endanger a few lives if someone in the area is on life support in some hospital or something. But then, he was the only one who seemed to have some doubts about the idea. So he kept his thoughts to himself.

Yeah, he didn't look so unkindly on dying in a blaze of gunfire, but he didn't like the idea of a totally stupid, pointless death. Like dying in a drunken shootout with an asshole like Jack, or getting gunned down by the cops while doing some totally stupid act of sabotage. Wasn't there a middle road here somewhere? His recent time with the little band of free spirited young people in Austin's "gang" had given him a glimmer of some more pleasant life. But was it available to someone like him?

He thought about his little encounter with Shelley over at the Dog House. She represented a version of the life his parents had led. Find a suitable mate, get a trade and a mortgage on a home, and then get busy raising a family. He didn't really disrespect that path in life. It sure was popular with a lot of people out there. Most of the people he knew, in fact. Just not Jack, or the people in this room with him tonight. What about Austin and her friends? Who knew where they were headed? A few more stupid decisions like the tree spiking and they might find themselves in a quiet cell near members of this "brigade". Yet there had seemed to be something different about their relation to the world and each other.

But why did he feel so fucked up? His dad had seen some pretty weird shit in the Second World War, but he'd seemed to be able to just suck it up. Not Skeeter though.

They spent the rest of the evening cleaning guns, studying the diagrams in *The Anarchist's Cookbook,* a book of very practical information about how to blow things up, and suggesting targets to each other. So this was how he would be spending his time for the foreseeable future. That is until the great revolution succeeds or they all end up in jail or dead.

It occurred to him that they really weren't as clever as they thought they were. They had readily accepted him on Peter's recommendation. But what did Peter really know about him? And that "job interview" at the restaurant, what had that proven? They were reckless and foolish in some obvious ways to an outsider. Just as they didn't seem to be able to make very sensible decisions about targets as a group, they didn't seem very capable of making very rational decisions about who to trust.

He could easily be an undercover cop. In fact, they could already have one or two cops in their collective already. How would they behave? They would do all they could to blend in. They would have a good story, like Skeeter's, and they would stick to it.

Maybe this really was the way revolutions were made. Reckless little groups of people. Fidel Castros, Che Guevarras, Mao Tse Tungs and Ho Chi Mins would foolishly plunge into revolutionary action. Screw up repeatedly, betray each other, get betrayed, get jailed repeatedly, some would die, and if time and history were on their side they would eventually succeed. He finally got it, the meaning of a quote from some young zealot in one of the New Left pamphlets in the bookstore: "We're gonna get our asses kicked, and we're gonna win!"

Was he ready for this? He spent most of the evening pondering that very question. Weighing things. Then he seemed to make a decision. He hung around until he could finally find an opportune moment to announce that he had to go check on his dog out in the truck. Once he was outside, he climbed in the truck, gave Rat Dog a quick pat. Then, just as he was about to start the engine and drive off, there was a tap at the window.

One of his new "comrades" stood at the truck window, peering in at him. "You weren't thinking of going anywhere were you?"

"No," Skeeter answered, as he slipped the truck keys back into his pocket.

"Why don't you bring your dog in. We've got a couple of bowls we can spare for his food and water."

"Okay." And the three of them headed for the door. Skeeter carried some of his gear and a bag of dry dog food for Rat Dog. His new comrades studied him a bit, when they thought he wasn't watching. They were friendly enough, but something had changed since his trip out to the truck.

Later that evening the group of them piled into an old black Buick that was parked around the back of the apartment building. Skeeter sat quietly wedged in between two comrades in the back seat. The well-tuned engine of the newer model Buick sedan purred quietly as they drove east on Roanoke and then turned left onto 10th Street heading south toward Capitol Hill. He was feeling a little nervous and a bit drowsy by the time they arrived at Broadway and pulled into a darkened parking lot just past Harvard Avenue.

"Okay, man, time to go into action," the guy next to him spoke, as he prodded him gently in the ribs as the car came to a stop. They got out and someone handed Skeeter a black cloth shopping bag. The lot was empty at this hour and no one was visible in the alley adjoining their parking spot. They were all dressed in dark clothes and wore stocking caps that were pulled down low enough to hide most of their features.

While one of them waited at the wheel in the car, two others slipped out to keep watch at either end of the dimly lit alley behind the building adjoining the parking lot. Skeeter and one other comrade then walked about halfway down the alley to where there was a window about five feet off the ground. They stood there for a few moments, until they got the signal from the others that it was safe to proceed. Then his partner gave Skeeter a quick boost up to the window, that was conveniently unlocked.

Skeeter climbed through the window and dropped to the floor below. He found himself in a small bathroom. Once inside he nervously fumbled with the cloth shopping bag, getting the mouth spread open, as moved out into the dark store. He was in a moderate sized grocery store that catered to a health conscious crowd. Skeeter immediately started "shopping" as he had been instructed, filling the shopping bag with a whole series of food items on a list. It took him about ten minutes to get everything they wanted.

Then he carried it all back to the bathroom and handed the bag out to the comrade who was waiting there for him. He was about to climb out, when he was suddenly told: "Duck back in!" And he had to wait there while the others scrambled away in the dark. He wasn't sure what to think. Was there someone coming? He waited for what seemed like an eternity. At one point a light shined into the window, illuminating a portion of the wall above his head. But after a tense moment, it moved on.

What was going on out there? Were they coming back for him? Maybe he was just regarded as expendable. If he was caught there, it wouldn't be all that much of a loss to them. But about then he got the signal to come, and he climbed out and closed the window behind him and the group of them hurried back to the car.

They drove around the block and parked on a side street just on the other side of Broadway next to a Safeway store. The driver laughed and said, "I thought I was gonna shit when I saw that pig car coming up behind me and turning into the alley. I almost accidentally leaned on the horn as I tried to slip as low as possible in the seat, so that they wouldn't see me."

"We got out of the alley at the far end just in time to make it look like we were just a group out for a late night walk to the tavern on the corner," said another. "Fuck, that was close," he said as a grin spread across his face

The tension had eased as they all piled out of the car for a late evening visit to the tavern for a beer and a burger. They crossed the street, laughing and joking, as Skeeter studied the billboard above the entrance to the tavern. There was a picture of a friendly looking, hairy old guy, who looked like he might easily be one of the homeless crowd out on the streets. Under the picture were the words: "Would you buy a burger cooked by this man? Hundreds have, and loved it!"

He had to admit that the guy did make a good burger as he contentedly ate one, wedged with his comrades into a narrow, little booth near the back of the dimly lit bar, with its stale, warm air and noisy coming and going of customers. He was feeling a bit of relief that things had worked out. The others seemed to thrive on the cheap thrill of getting away with it. He wasn't so sure himself.

About then, one of them turned to him, probably noticing the slightly troubled look on his face. "This was just a warm up, man. Wait 'til you see what we've got planned." And he winked pleasantly as he took another sip from his mug of beer.

Then the group of them started talking about the pros and cons of robbing a bank they had been scoping out on the outskirts of town. Right there in the bar, with all these people sitting nearby. Were they crazy? He wanted payback for some of the things that had happened to him that he blamed on the fucked up system. But these people, what did they want? Cheap thrills and notoriety? We're they just bored with their lives? He listened in silence as they discussed how quickly and easily they might be in and out of the bank. Were there easy escape routes, and how likely were the pigs to be anywhere in the vicinity? It was just a matter of time, thought Skeeter, before members of this crew would be sitting in a cell next to some of their kindred spirits, over in Walla Walla Prison. That is, if they didn't end up dead in a shoot out with the cops. And he had thought that the U.S. army was full of wackos. Welcome to the civilian world.

When they returned to their car it was well past midnight. Skeeter thought they might be ready to return home, but no, the driver turned to the others and announced with a devilish grin, "how about a little midnight rambling, folks?"

"Sure, man, what you got in mind?" Asked a comrade.

"I think in honor of our soldier boy here, we go pay a visit to a soft target military installation."

"Oh, and what's that?" Someone asked.

"ROTC building on the UW campus."

"Cool, man. Let's do it." And they crossed Capital Hill and entered the University of Washington campus from University Village. It was all happening so quickly that Skeeter had trouble even processing the information. What were they up to now? The driver pulled the car up alongside a dormitory at the top of the hill just inside of the campus. He parked in among some students' cars and killed the engine. Then he turned to Skeeter.

"You're gonna go for a little walk with your brother here," and he pointed to the guy next to Skeeter. "There are some tools you two will want in the trunk. See you back here in about ten minutes."

The two of them got out of the car, and his "brother" rummaged around in the trunk until he found some things he wanted and stuffed them into a backpack. He handed Skeeter a pair of thin, black leather gloves to put on and put a pair on as well. Then they set off in the direction of the ROTC building, a block away. Skeeter was totally clueless about what was to happen next. And it was all happening so fast that he had no time to do anything but follow orders.

When they were in position, in a dark patch of shrubbery on one side of the building where it adjoined a neighboring building, his comrade pulled out the makings of a Molotov cocktail and handed it to Skeeter. He pulled the cork out of a quart-sized bottle filled with a flammable mixture of laundry detergent and some fuel. He stuffed a rag in the top with a corner hanging out and handed it to Skeeter.

Then he pulled a cigarette lighter out of his pocket and picked up a sizeable rock from a nearby landscaped garden bed. "I'm going to smash the window with this rock. Then you get ready to toss the cocktail as soon as I light it for you. Ready?"

Skeeter could not believe that this was happening, but it was coming at him so fast that he barely had time to do anything but react to the demands of the moment. With his eyes fixed on the bottle in his trembling hand, he nodded, and after a quick survey of the surrounding area to see that no one was coming their way, his comrade hurled the rock and the window shattered with what sounded like a crash loud enough to be heard blocks away.

Skeeter waited anxiously as his partner pulled out the lighter and lit the rag. Then he hurled the Molotov cocktail through the shattered window. There was something eerily déjà vu about all of this. Had he done this before? No. But there was something both exhilarating and even a bit satisfying about it. Yeah, wasn't this exactly what he had been hoping to do?

As they heard the cocktail crash to the floor inside the building, his comrade shouted, "Let's go, man!" And the two of them ran as fast as they could, back to the waiting car, now idling at the nearest street corner.

They were already down the hill and disappearing into the small stream of traffic alongside the University Village shopping center when they heard the first siren of a police car sound. Skeeter was still breathing hard from the run to the car, and his heart hadn't yet returned to normal as they sped off into the night, laughing at what they'd managed to pull off with little effort or planning.

It occurred to Skeeter that breaking the rules of society and getting away with it was easier than most people imagined. There wasn't a cop behind every tree, and most of the time spontaneous mischief making had no real consequences. That is, until it did, because repeat actions like those he had participated in that night, no doubt, would eventually end in capture by the authorities. Just that night alone the charges of burglary and arson could have landed them in jail for a substantial time. Was he ready for this? It looked like he had already jumped in with both feet. At least this time the gang did head for home and bed.

Skeeter was nudged awake about four in the morning by a wet, little muzzle. When he saw who it was, he gave him a little stroke behind the ears and began to think about all that had occurred in the past twenty four hours. Then, quickly, and as quietly as possible, he slipped his clothes on and led the little dog out of the bedroom. They wove their way carefully around the sleeping bodies spread out on the carpeted floor in the living room.

Suddenly a comrade opened his eyes and looked right up at the figure of Skeeter, standing alongside him. He stood there, paralyzed with fear. It was all over. There would be no escaping the group, and who knows what hell he would pay for this second attempt to get away from them? Then, as quickly as he had opened his eyes and stared up at Skeeter, he closed them again, and rolled over onto his side and fell back asleep.

Rat Dog stood by the door, looking back at Skeeter expectantly. If nothing else, the dog needed to go out and pee. He suddenly whined, just a little whimper, but it was enough to awaken another member of the gang. "What's that? What's goin' on?" He mumbled.

"Nothing," whispered Skeeter in the comrade's ear. "Dog just needs to go out and take a piss."

That seemed to satisfy him, and he too went back to sleep. Skeeter started moving toward the door again, as quietly as possible. He slipped the chain on the door and he and Rat Dog were out in the hall.

Would they make it out of here without being caught this time? The dog seemed to sense the need for stealth, since he didn't utter a sound as they made their way down the hall and out into the night air. It was the hour when the city was as close to asleep as it ever got. There was still the sound of the occasional truck or car out on the tall freeway bridge over Portage Bay, but mostly it was calm and peaceful out on the street as they climbed into the truck.

There was nothing very quiet about the truck engine as he started it up. Then he heard the voice. "Hey, where do you think you're going?" And then he saw his comrade with a pistol in his hand, approaching the truck. Skeeter grabbed the shotgun from behind the seat and poked the muzzle of the gun out the window and let off a shot into the air.

As the guy with the gun ducked to the ground at the sound of the explosion, they sped off in the direction of the wooded parkway to the south. Skeeter couldn't help but glance into the rear view mirror every few moments, watching for the telltale signs of a car coming after them. But none appeared, and after another half hour on the freeway and then cruising down the Mukilteo Speedway, they finally arrived back at the Mukilteo ferry dock, in time to catch the first ferry of the morning run, back to the island.

He and Rat Dog drove back in to the cabin and Skeeter stumbled wearily into the chill, dank, uninviting room and flopped down on the bed. He had the shotgun lying loaded and ready beside him on the bare mattress. The small pistol was in easy reach beside his head. Rat Dog climbed up beside him and wedged his small back up against Skeeter's and promptly fell asleep. Sleep didn't come to Skeeter quite so easily. As he thought about the past few weeks, and then thought about his life for this past year, it seemed to him like everything he had touched had turned to shit.

Later that morning he made a trip out to the Greenbank Store, where he picked up a copy of the Seattle Post Intelligencer. On page three he found what he was looking for, a brief police report that an attempt was made the night before to set fire to the ROTC building on the University of

Washington campus. Apparently the incendiary device landed on a bare concrete floor in an empty storage room. The fire was contained to a small area and did minimal damage to the building. Police were conducting an investigation.

Skeeter wasn't sure if he was disappointed or relieved at the outcome of the attack. It all happened so quickly, and he knew that he didn't want anymore to do with the gang that involved him in the action. But it seemed like this was one of those cases of "be careful what you wish for." He was now more confused than ever about what he did and did not wish for. But what recent events had done was kindle a new feeling in him that he was just barely aware of. He wanted to survive it all. Although he wasn't quite sure how or why. He spent the rest of that day roaming the woods with Rat Dog and just mulling over his options.

Chapter Nine

Skeeter arrived at the communal house about nine o'clock that night. Ross, Austin and the others peered out the window, a little surprised to see Skeeter. Ross actually looked slightly pleased to see them both again so soon. "Hi, all," he said as he approached the half open front door. "I've got a little situation that I was wondering if you folks might help me with." And Skeeter explained his problem with Jack, and asked if there might be a way for him to lay low for awhile out here with them. "I just need the guy to cool down a bit before I go back to staying at my place, That's all," he lied. "If I could lay a sleeping bag down out in your barn. That would be enough."

After hearing him out, the group talked about it among themselves while Skeeter waited out in the truck. "He's kind of a strange dude," said Carl. "But he did keep us from getting caught."

"Yeah, but he isn't really one of us, just one of the local yokels. So he smokes a little weed once in a while. That doesn't make him cool. And we don't need his kind of trouble. Sounds like kind of a jerk, smacking some guy just because he pissed him off. Let him solve his own problems. He's the one who got himself into this mess. Let him get himself out of it," Annie argued.

"It wouldn't be that much of a big deal if we let him crash for a while in that shed out back that we set up for extra people who show up," said Ross. "If it isn't working out, we can just tell him to leave."

"That sounds okay to me," said Carl. "He can help us out with some of the chores, including the gardening and the firewood."

"I don't know. This guy just seems like trouble. And we don't really know him," said Austin. "But if you guys really want to help him out, it's okay with me."

"And he is kind of cute," said Carl, with a little giggle. "That is, if you were to clean him up a little." Which made Austin roll her eyes.

They called Skeeter and Rat Dog into the house and told him their decision. He stowed his old truck in the back of the old barn, and then he came in and sat down at the table where they were all about to have a late supper. Then, just as they had the last time he had been here, they all joined hands and sat in silence, making the moment special.

He was a little more comfortable with the ritual this time. He just tried to breathe, take it in and let it out, and to feel the warmth of the hands that held his. 'I could really use some shelter from the shit storm out there, waiting to rain down on me,' he thought to himself as he tried to get into the spirit of their moment of silent prayer.

After the meal Austin guided him out to the shed. It was just a dingy little storage shed with one small, cracked window. It had been swept out and an old mattress had been laid out on a low wooden pallet. There was a candle set in a tin can filled with sand near the bed. Skeeter tossed his own bedding on top of the mattress and spread Rat Dog's old blanket out next to the bed. He was careful to keep his guns well hidden, knowing that none of this crowd would relate well to the idea of his having them here. They appeared to go around unarmed. Which seemed just plain nuts to Skeeter.

All the same, as he looked around, he thought to himself: 'This will do. It will have to.' Not like he had a lot of options at the moment. Rat Dog seemed to be happy though. Austin had him on her lap as she sat leaning her back against the far wall of the eight by ten foot cabin, scratching him under the chin. "Why do you call him Rat Dog?" She asked, as the little black mutt peered adoringly up at her.

"Just because he turned out to be good at hunting down rats around my cabin."

"Oh," she said, obviously not very impressed by his lack of imagination or endearment in the naming of his dog. "So you okay with this place?" She asked as she set the dog down and began to stand up.

"I should be good out here. Actually I ain't so keen about being around those two fairy boys in the house," he confided in her.

"Well, some of the folks here aren't so thrilled about having you around either," she responded, her eyes flashing in obvious displeasure. "Though Carl finds you kind of cute," she added.

He hesitated, not sure what to make of that comment. But he felt like he had to say something, so he plunged on. "I don't have anything against those guys, but it really creeps me out thinking about what they do together."

"Then don't think about it. They probably don't want to think about what you do either. So you're probably even. Live and let live."

"Yeah, I guess..." He mumbled.

"Catch you in the morning," and she slipped out the door into the cool, dark night, leaving them there in their respective beds with a dim candle flame flickering and casting a pale glow over the weathered gray boards of the shed. There was a faint hush of breeze in the big cottonwood tree a little south of the house. He could also hear the faint, deep croak of a solitary, old toad hidden somewhere near the shed. It seemed a little early in the year for him to come out of hibernation and announce himself, but there were already some faint signs of the coming spring.

Even though he was in this odd place with a group of near strangers, Skeeter felt a certain amount of familiar comfort here. He was surrounded by familiar sounds and smells. He had his dog with him, and this was still his island, if not among his usual haunts on the 55 mile long island. And he had the pistol he'd bought, hidden under the blanket in easy reach of his hand. He found that fact a bit comforting, given that he had decided to hide within easy reach of Jack, if he should ever figure out where Skeeter was.

He slept better than he had in a while, though he was startled awake twice in the night by bad dreams. When he finally awoke, it was to the sound of a rooster crowing nearly in his ear. Rat Dog was barking at the sound, and there was no way Skeeter was going to get any more sleep. He could see sunshine infused with dust from the room pouring through the south facing window. He slid out of bed and dressed in the narrow sliver of light that provided some small warmth in the otherwise frigid room. Rat Dog was anxiously pawing at the door, in need of an outdoor area to water.

They stepped outside into bright sunlight and a refreshing breeze coming in off Useless Bay. Rat Dog peed while Skeeter surveyed the scene. The old farmhouse was a bit worse for wear, but it seemed little changed from the place he had visited occasionally as a kid. There was still an old tire hanging from a rope tied to the limb of a big walnut tree. A country kid's swing set. The farmhouse could use a coat of paint, but that was the case back when it was a family farm. Now what was it? The present crew wasn't exactly a family, and they seemed like they were just dinking around with farming. They had a dairy goat in a pen near the house and there were maybe a dozen laying hens in the old coop. The garden seemed a little small, but it looked like they were trying to do it all by hand. In fact, there was no sign of a tractor or tiller. It looked like they were letting the old hay fields turn to fallow meadow land. The old orchard had received a little pruning that winter, but it didn't seem like they had taken enough of the new growth, especially the sucker branches off. City kids, no doubt, but they were learning.

He knocked at the back door. Carl opened it for him with a sweet smile on his face. Thinks I'm kind of cute, eh? Thought Skeeter as he nodded in return. What is this queer stuff all about, he wondered. Don't these guys get turned on by women's bodies? I mean, how is that not possible? And what is there to see that's cute in men? Maybe the term gay sort of fits these guys though. They seem sort of cheerful anyway.

There were several people sitting around the table eating home made crunchy granola with some of the farm's goat milk yogurt over it. He was more of a bacon and eggs sort of guy himself, but the bowl of breakfast cereal he was offered was actually not bad. The table was made from three broad pine planks with a slightly polished look from the satin varnish finish. The bowls were also made of wood, probably with a walnut oil seasoning on them. They had kind of a nice feel to them, and he much preferred them to the cheap, soft plastic bowls he'd been using in his cabin.

As they ate, they talked about what to do that day. There was a shopping trip that Austin and Annie would do. Ross and Skeeter would work on firewood. Hal and Carl had a short term paying job over at the Holly Farm on Holmes Harbor north of Freeland. Here it was only his first day with them, and Skeeter was already plugging in to their communal life. And it wasn't long before he and Rat Dog were part of the everyday life of the communal farm.

That first Sunday he was introduced to another ritual among this gang. After breakfast they all gathered in the farm living room and took up comfortable seats around the room. They invited Skeeter to join them, if he liked. They were going to have an hour long "silent meeting." It was part of a Quaker practice, something that strange little religious group had apparently made central to their religion for some three hundred years.

He declined to join them. It was all a bit too strange. Why on earth would a group of people ever want to just sit in a room together without saying a word, and for an entire fucking hour? He would later learn that they didn't actually always keep their mouths shut for a whole hour. If somebody really thought they had a sufficiently "spiritual" gem of a thought to share with others, they might just spit it out.

All the same, it weirded him out a little, to find out that he had stumbled into a strange little bunch of hippies who were into all sorts of stuff. He later found out that they liked to do yoga together at times, and practice Buddhist meditation. They just picked all this shit up from people they met, and then adopted this or that practice, because they found it cool. Whatever, he thought. None of his business, what they did. And they were putting him up, no small thing.

Two weeks passed on the farm. March became April, Skeeter woke each day to the first crowing of the rooster. He wiped the sleep out of his eyes and nudged the dog off the edge of the bed. If it had been a cool night, Rat Dog would have wedged himself tight against Skeeter's back for warmth. Once he was fully awake he would be whining to be let out to pee.

Skeeter usually also slipped around the edge of the shed, out of view of the house, and joined the dog in this. That particular morning he realized that for the first time he had forgotten to grab the little pistol and tuck it into his belt, hidden away under his open shirt tail. Unbeknownst to the others, he carried it with him everywhere he went. He thought about what a bummer it would be if Jack came around the corner right then, and caught him in the middle of a pee. Why did he always have to be on his mind? He was the last person he wanted to think about, but he was always plaguing his thoughts. Maybe a braver person would just live his life and come what may. There was the old saying: "a brave man dies but once, while a coward dies a thousand deaths." The coward always living in fear and dread.

Then they walked slowly toward the house. This was Skeeter's favorite time of day. It was as if the world was made new each day as the sun rose. He loved the feeling of the fresh, clean morning air in his lungs, and the chatter of the birds just stirring from their sleep, and the lovely glowing shades of green all around him, of grass and shrubs and tree boughs. He started humming a song from one of the records in the farm collection, and then the words came to him: "Morning has broken, like the first morning, blackbird has spoken, like the first bird. Praise for creation, praise every morning, God's re-creation of the new day..."

There was the delicious smell of pancakes cooking on the stove top, and the radio, as usual, was tuned to the public station KRAB and Stu Witmer was playing his usual odd mix of world music. This morning it was the Tibetan monkey chant. Annie was the cook this morning.

She was a somewhat small but sturdy ragamuffin of a young woman. She liked to wear some of the natural cotton and woolen clothes favored by this crowd, with just a touch of color, in something like a peasant babushka. He thought that the farm girls were kind of strange for their avoidance of make up, jewelry or other adornment. But over time he grew comfortable with the natural simplicity of it. Not unlike some of the traditional conservative religious folk, he supposed, such as Amish, Mennonites or Quakers, maybe. She was quite the cook, and these buckwheat cakes with honey and butter smeared on top were one of her specialties.

Communal breakfast, and later supper, were especially pleasant times of the day for him. There was always lots of joking and kidding around, along with some serious discussion about what they would do that day. They would hatch plans about how to earn money, and who would tend to chores, and the like. Evenings more often were given over to play. Then there was music and wine or weed, and some free form, silly dance, especially the girls seemed to like to do that, and walks in the evening woods or along the beach, watching the stars, listening to the waves splashing on the sandy shore, catching glimpses of the mostly elusive wildlife, the deer, the foxes, the occasional otter, or the owls, or the ever present seabirds, the gulls, loons, geese and ducks.

This particular morning it was decided that the group would plant potatoes and peas in their garden. Skeeter was designated to guide the work, given his farm background. They hand tilled the soil with garden spades. It had a dark brown appearance, somewhat loose and sandy despite the addition of aged cow manure last fall. It gave off a faint familiar odor of the fungi in forest duff. They dug deep furrows and Skeeter followed after and laid cut potatoes at six inch intervals, and someone else buried the row. Then they created long, narrow shallow trenches with garden hoes, and he spread a generous line of peas in each one. They spent the rest of the morning preparing ground for the eventual sowing of greens such as spinach, chard and lettuce, and additional sowings of the overwintering kale, cabbage and broccoli.

Because the Maritime Pacific Northwest climate was so mild, most years they would only get a couple of hard freezes that might last a week at most, certain greens could be harvested all winter and into the spring. The kids at the farm had an overwintering patch of kale, broccoli, cabbage and chard that they would harvest. Skeeter was impressed by the fact that they supplemented this with the harvest of the first stinging nettles that had emerged in the woods and meadows. Not too many people knew that they made a tasty side dish that tasted a lot like spinach when cooked.

Of course, these gardeners were strictly organic, referring to the Rodale Garden Books for guidance. It seemed a little extreme to Skeeter, who thought that if some of the latest technology, including chemical inputs for farming, could make life a little easier, why not take advantage of them? But he knew that some of the old farmers from the island also viewed chemical use in agriculture with suspicion, and he respected their experience. It wouldn't be the first time that new didn't necessarily mean better.

Chapter Ten

The farm had occasional guests, mostly young people who shared their values. Free spirits, often recent arrivals, but some homegrown, would join them for evening gatherings. Skeeter mostly kept his distance, retreating to the shed with Rat Dog. But sometimes he couldn't resist the temptation to listen in and hear what they were doing.

The farm crowd was always taking up some cause or other. If it wasn't saving the trees or opposing oil pipelines planned to cross the island, it was some other cause Skeeter had never heard of before. The list seemed endless. He sometimes just wanted to say, "Get a life!" Didn't they have anything better to do than poke their noses in other people's business? He himself, however, took the Vietnam War very personally, but who could argue that it hadn't gotten very personal when he was wounded?

There was one of their causes that captured his own interest. He stood just inside the kitchen, mostly out of view of the visitors, when a crowd came by one evening that was campaigning to create an owner builder amendment to the county building code. As one slightly stocky and bulldog stubborn leader of the campaign, who had milled his own lumber from his own land and built a sturdy little, illegal house for his family, explained to the gathering: "It would allow people who did all of the work themselves to act as their own contractor. An owner builder can save a lot of money and create an original house to his liking. As long as they met some minimal health and safety regs, rural folk whose houses had no effect on neighbors, could use this law to their benefit."

His slim, pretty little wife, who might have actually been the real brains behind the effort, chimed in: "What we're asking for is a county wide referendum on the amendment."

Government officials apparently hated the idea. So did contractors who made their money off people dependent on them for their building needs. Here was one of those issues that appealed to a lot of conservative country folk and a free spirited, back to the country crowd of new young folks. Skeeter really liked the idea. It already matched the philosophy of a lot of the county's rural, self-sufficient population. They always had preferred to "make do or do it yourself." And when government wanted to

snoop into their business for tax or regulation purposes, they usually took
the approach: 'Better to ask forgiveness for something the government
might not approve of, than go in asking government permission ahead of
time.'

Now a big guy, who together with his Georgia peach of a partner,
were building their own log house with telephone pole size logs that they
were cutting and peeling off their own land, got up to speak. "Get behind
this, it'll help a lot of people," he urged. Man of few words, thought
Skeeter. But good ones. He wondered a little about the huge logs they were
cutting, if you're not careful, one of those things can fall on you, and that
could really hurt.

But he liked what a lively, entertaining crowd this was. Like the
little guy with the beard and wire rim glasses, who supposedly lived in a
homemade yurt somewhere back in Skeeter's own neck of the woods. He
and his blond, little honey, besides the usual flock of chickens and a dairy
goat, had a donkey, who hauled loads in and out of their woods by way of
a foot trail that was the only access to their homestead. What a bunch.
What was there not to like about these latest arrivals to his island.

There was no doubt in Skeeter's mind that those who ran the local
government and the crowd that paid for their election would do everything
they could to destroy this amendment to the building code. It could pass,
but it won't last long, he was thinking. But, hell, you had to admire the
spunk of these folks.

There was something happening to the world around him. It felt
like a bulldozer was loose, crushing all in its path. He was beginning to
notice all the money to be made off helpless consumers. It seemed to spell
the end of the existence of a sparse, self-reliant population of free people
on the land here. He saw the signs all around him of the demise of the rural
way of life of the island. People in charge often paid lip service to retaining
the rural character of the county. Everybody seemed to love that idea. But
all most of them wanted was the spread of the city luxuries, conveniences
and lifestyle. Their ideal vision of country life was a big suburban home in
a picture perfect setting of manicured lawns and landscaping framed by
mountain and water views.

And too many of those that earned their living indoors, with no
heavy lifting, saw those who worked the land as nothing more than chumps

and losers. If you were too stupid to join the suit and tie crowd, you were liable to be regarded as no more than a human beast of burden. They might use your strong back to do the menial tasks around their luxury homes, but they had no use for rural people who did not serve their needs.

The local people who still hunted and fished and grew much of their own food, built their own homes, repaired their own cars and machinery, and had little indebtedness were of no real use to the well-heeled. And there were subtle ways to rid the county of them. Condemn their old houses. Tax them off the land. Impose rules on them that would make their lifestyle untenable.

Yet, here were young, idealistic refugees from the modern American dream, who respected many of the old country ways, and the old Jeffersonian ideal of free, self sufficient, country folk. And they had a land ethic that you couldn't help but admire. The farm crew had recently visited one example of this at the new Chinook Learning Center out near where Skeeter's family lived. The folks they met out there talked about "nature and spirit" in relation to land and community. Their vision of the world seemed a little "airy fairy" to Skeeter. But then the way they were settling in on their rural property struck him as being like a small corner of the "peaceable kingdom" where the "lion would lie down with the lamb" talk of the Bible. Deer, rabbits, chipmunks, squirrels and a dozen different species of birds calmly went about their lives amidst the quiet, gentle people of the place.

There came a day though, when they had some visitors to the farm that he didn't enjoy one bit. They came after he had been at the farm for about a month. The visitors showed up rather unexpectedly from the city. They drove up that day in a dirty, old Ford Econoline van with darkened windows. Ross greeted the visitors first, approaching the van and calling out someone's name, someone he obviously knew. But when Skeeter saw them, even from a fair distance, while working in the old orchard, he knew who they were, and he began plotting in his mind how to slip off into the woods as quietly as possible and get away.

He saw Austin peering out from the doorway of the main house at the visitors. Then she frowned, as she too appeared to recognize them. Skeeter peered cautiously through the brush. Yes, it was definitely his "old friends" from the city. How in the hell did Ross know them? And why were they here? Austin also apparently knew them, but not with any fondness, because she stalked off, finding some things to do elsewhere on the farm.

Skeeter's first impulse was to run, but then, as he thought about it a bit, he decided that he was more curious than afraid. As they visited for a while in the kitchen over tea, Skeeter continued watching from the far end of the orchard. Was Ross right now telling them about Skeeter's presence on the farm? Was that right, were they really here to find him? Why else would they be here?? Hadn't he also pissed them off, and wasn't he probably on their enemies' list as well now?

He made his way around the house under the cover of the spring foliage of salmonberry and elderberry bushes and slipped into the shed, Rat Dog close on his heels. He nervously pulled the shotgun out of his bedding and felt to be sure that the small pistol was still in his belt. His hand trembled slightly as he fed a shell into the open chamber of the gun. Then, locking Rat Dog in, he hurried out to the barn, where he peered out through a crack in the door, waiting for them to come look for him.

His mouth felt dry, and his stomach fluttered in nervous anticipation of the confrontation to come. They were probably learning the details about how best to jump him right now. If he hadn't been seen, they would probably go to the shed first, and he could probably get off a few shots from the barn before they knew where it was coming from. He had released the safety on the shotgun and his finger rested lightly on the trigger with the barrel pointed at the ground.

But the group of them, accompanied by Ross when they eventually emerged from the house, headed directly for the van. The gang climbed in and began to slowly drive away. Ross waved to them as they drove off. Skeeter, now far more curious than afraid, waited only a brief minute and then jumped into his truck and followed them out at a safe distance. They made their way north on the highway, past the old Freeland founder's house and the boat yard, then turned left onto Bush Point Road. After a couple miles the road curved to the right and then continued north to the old county gravel pit off Smugglers Cove Road near Lagoon Point.

It was kind of creepy having this bunch out here on the island, thought Skeeter. But he felt a bit relieved knowing that he had them in his sights, rather than the other way around. That was always good when dealing with a car load of guys armed to the teeth, especially guys who might have a grudge against you. Lucky for him that they didn't cross paths at the farm. He would have been most decidedly outgunned.

The city crew really did have a decent set of pistols and rifles. These included some rifles with semi-automatic capabilities, due to tampering with the firing mechanism. Skeeter's old shotgun would not have performed quite so well in any firefight with the guests. For a little while it must have sounded like World War Three was breaking out as the group blasted away at targets set up on one sandy hillside of the old pit.

After the guests were clearly on their way to the ferry dock in order to depart for the city, Skeeter returned to the farm and hid his truck back in the barn. Then he went into the house and asked Ross who the guests were. "Oh, just a friend from my old communal house on Capital Hill in Seattle with some people he knows. They're kind of weird. They dig what the SLA did down in California. I think that they may have some sort of ties to the GJB in Seattle. They sure talk enough about them."

"GJB?" he asked in feigned ignorance.

"George Jackson Brigade. You've heard of them, haven't you?"

"I guess," Skeeter answered. He really did not want to talk more about the guests after all.

"Well, they seem to know a lot about you. They kept asking me questions. Whether I had ever met you. Did I know where you lived. That sort of thing."

Skeeter's throat grew tight. He knew what his next question had to be. "And what did you say?"

"Told them I'd never heard of you, and no idea where they could find you." He paused and said, "So what did you do to piss them off?"

Skeeter thought about that, then finally answered. "Not much really. Just decided that what they were into wasn't for me."

About then Carl passed through the house on his way out to a little shop he had set up out in the barn. He had seen Carl playing with some big metal boxy thing. Some electronic gizmo. "What's that?" he had asked in passing.

"Oh, just some new electronic kit, based on some recent technology for a kind of computing and word processing, being developed by some guys I know. I've been interested in this stuff for a while. I recently got an offer to join them in putting together a company over in Redmond, where they are working on some stuff like this to sell. Maybe I will. It's really interesting."

"Oh, yeah?" Weird guy, thought Skeeter, as he headed out the back door.

Later that evening when he had a chance to catch Ross by himself again, he said to him, "Ross, what do you really know about those guys that came by this afternoon?"

"Not much, really."

"Well, I know too much about them, and now they're after me, all because I wanted payback for some shit. It was just plain stupid of me."

"Really..." Was all that Ross could think to say.

As Skeeter returned to his shed he wondered if this was the last he would see of the Seattle gang. Were they after him now because he knew too much about them? If the cops somehow got ahold of him he could tell them a whole lot about the group. So what would they do if they caught up with him? Just threaten him? Kill him? Then again, he had participated in crimes with them. They could snitch on him as well. If they go down, he goes down too. Was that part of the point of rushing him into action with them?

So was this the kind of world that armed revolution inhabited? Not much different than the world of organized crime. Would we be any better off if they took power?

It was a clear, cool night. There were a million stars sparkling like diamonds through the thin foliage of the trees behind the house. Here he was, so mired in his own troubled thoughts, while the vast, magnificent universe was out there, all around him, totally indifferent to him and his problems. He looked up into that incredible night sky and wondered how anyone could not feel a sense of wonder, an awe, when he stared up at that mysterious, yet so prosaic, commonplace sight.

Not too long ago he had been unable to notice that star-filled sky. But now he reveled in the sight. He just wanted out of these stupid games with violent people that he'd somehow gotten himself into. But how? Even his sleep was haunted by nightmares of those who wanted to make his life hell. If it wasn't Jack chasing him around and beating on him as a kid, it

was a Viet Cong mortar shell coming out of nowhere and blowing his
world all to hell, and now it included a new bunch.

And there was one other group that haunted his dreams that he had
never told anyone about. Army basic training had consisted of a deliberate
process of breaking a person down and then creating in him a sense of utter
loyalty and devotion to those labeled his "superiors." These were people
with absolute life and death power over the recruit. They told him when to
get up, when to eat, when to sleep and just about everything else he would
do in the course of the day. They were to be obeyed without question or
hesitation. The demands of war created this need for absolute surrender of
power to ones superiors.

The process sometimes involved a cruelty and barbarity that
haunted Skeeter to the present day. There were always weaker and stronger
men in any unit. And the strongest among them were assigned roles as
enforcers of the commands of their superiors. The weakest among them
were subjected to considerable ridicule and scorn, and on occasion much
worse.

There was one night that he will never be able to get out of his
mind, when a group of men decided to teach a lesson to a weak and
vulnerable recruit. Clare Cargile was this wimpy, chubby little guy who
could never keep up with the rest of the unit. He readily cried like a girl
when he was hurt, and he dragged the whole unit down in training.

The method employed by the group of men who took it upon
themselves to eliminate him from their ranks would haunt Skeeter forever
after. If it wasn't exactly gang rape, the brute force used on him was the
psychological equivalent. About one in the morning a group of recruits
shoved Cargile's head inside of a pillow case. Then the group of them
dragged him into a storage closet and began to work him over.

At first Skeeter imagined that maybe they would just rough him up
a bit, but as the muffled cries for help grew more desperate and anguished,
he knew that something more terrible was happening just a dozen feet
away from the silent rows of men in their bunks. It seemed to go on
forever. Every minute that passed felt like an eternity.

Although he didn't participate, he became an accomplice through
his silence about the incident. Clare disappeared after that. Skeeter and
some others at the bottom of the pecking order in the unit lived in constant

fear, occasionally reinforced by threats, that they could be next, if they didn't watch out. No, Skeeter did not sleep well since returning from the service. And he liked to keep a weapon close at hand at all times, in case he needed to defend himself. Again that night the shotgun lay cradled in his arms and the pistol lay within easy reach just above his head.

Chapter Eleven

Skeeter and Rat Dog fell into a daily routine on the farm. Although he had occasional opportunities to sneak off the place, Skeeter was mostly content to stay put. Others also seemed willing to enable him to do this, doing shopping and other off farm chores. In addition to farm chores, he took it upon himself to do a certain amount of maintenance and repair around the farm. Everything from a tune up on the old VW bug to repair of rain gutters on the house. So he felt like a useful member of the household despite his reluctance to venture off the farm.

In his spare time he found himself interested in reading the books in the farm library. While he found some of the practical books such as guides to gardening or dairy goats useful, he really became intrigued by some of the other topics. He became absorbed for a time in the reading of Joseph Heller's novel, *Catch 22,* and then Ken Kesey's *One Flew Over the Cuckoo's Nest*. He had already read a few of the books about radical political philosophy and activism.

He had discovered that he really enjoyed reading books. Howard Zinn's *Peoples' History of the United States* still seemed like the real eye opener to him. He had heard rumors about Chinese settlers of the Coupeville area, early in the century, being chased out by their European white neighbors. And there were ugly incidents even in Langley in more recent times, when Black visitors to the island were chased off by bigoted local folks. And the Native Indian population, those that had survived the plague of European diseases, had been shunted off to squalid, little reservations on Puget Sound and treated as second class citizens. You didn't have to travel to the Deep South, the former land of Black slavery and recent terrorism by the KKK, to find the ugly face of White Supremacy and racism.

He was more than willing to let Austin take responsibility for Rat Dog's visit to the vet for a rabies booster shot, when she suggested it one day. He had plenty to do on the farm, and she seemed to like to give attention to his little mutt. Several hours later she and the dog returned and joined him in the farm kitchen.

"Bad news," she said as she sat down across from him at the kitchen table. "Rat Dog was spotted by that guy Jack when I was leaving

Payless after shopping. He came up to the car and stared in the window at your dog. Then he tapped on my window and asked, 'where did you get that dog?' I told him I found him roaming around the woods near our house, but I'm not sure that he believed me."

She looked anxiously at Skeeter as she said all of this, reflecting the worry on his own face. "I guess we'll just have to hope that he believed you..." Skeeter tried to reassure her, but he actually had expected the day to come, sooner or later, when he would be found out. That Jack would find out that he hadn't really left the island. He had even told his parents that he and Rat Dog were going to go off on a trip for a while and that he would call them once in a while, which he had failed to do.

However, the spring days passed rather uneventfully. Blossom season came and went among the wild plum and cherry trees in the forests, followed by the succession of blooms among the orchard trees. The alders lost their reddish brown appearance as the catkins all dropped to the ground and the trees filled out in pale green foliage. The grass grew tall in the fields. The season for eating steamed wild nettle greens and oyster mushrooms gave way to the season of cultivated greens from the garden.

There were days, however, that were anything but routine. One evening the group anguished over what to do with the young buck goat, born that winter, that was beginning to get rambunctious. The goat wasn't likely to be of value for breeding purposes or much else.

Skeeter finally said, "well, why don't you just eat the goat then."

The others looked at him, a little startled by the idea. They weren't vegetarians, but they hadn't butchered anything bigger than a chicken since coming to the farm. They got a lot of their knowledge of things like chickens or goats from books they owned.

"But we've never slaughtered or butchered an animal before," said Ross.

"I can show you how to do it. I've done it enough times," offered Skeeter.

"Okay," said Austin. "But I don't want it to be just some mindless act. We're going to thank the animal's spirit first," she announced.

Skeeter rolled his eyes. "Sure. Whatever..."

The next day Skeeter prepared for the slaughter. He had considered just using the 22 pistol to put a bullet in the back of the goat's head, but finally settled on slitting its throat with a sharp knife. He smiled to himself as he sharpened the knife. Fucking wimpy city kids. They need a ceremony to thank the goat before they can deal with the death. Pathetic.

He brought his tools into the barn where the goat and the farm crew waited for him. The goat was a white Saanen and Alpine mix with foot long horns that curved slightly back toward the goat's shoulders. He was tied to a railing and eating contentedly on some alfalfa hay.

When Skeeter approached the group they made way for him. Then as he grasped the rope around the goat's neck, Austin spoke, "wait, let's form a circle around the goat and take each other's hands." Skeeter shrugged and then stepped away from the goat to join hands with the others. It all seemed a bit silly to him, but when he saw the serious expressions on the faces of the others, he tried not to show any disrespect for their feelings. Then Austin began to recite something she'd composed for this moment:

Gentle beast,
We took it upon ourselves to aid your entrance
into this world,
and so now we must also be party to your leaving it.
There is no further place for you
to grow older in this world.
The wild world of your ancestors
holds no place for you,
and you will be less kindly received
among humans as a full grown buck.
The time has come for your goat spirit
to return to the mystery beyond life
each of us goes to in our time.
Thank you for coming
to our beckoning call.
Forgive us for your leaving,
also at our request.
Your spirit enriched the world,
and we were pleased to know you.
Your meat after death

will still contain much of the energy
that danced and schemed
and baa-ed through life.
We will take this energy into ourselves
to be transformed into human dances,
dreams, schemes and songs,
until your goat spirit returns
in the births of next spring.

Skeeter's impatience had diminished. He had to admit that even he felt a bit bad when some vibrant, living creature became a dead lump of meat during the hunt. The native people had always asked an animal's spirit for some forgiveness for their turning a fellow creature into a meal. It felt somehow more fitting and even a bit comforting, what Austin had done. These Nature Kids still held some surprises for him.

Near the end of May the farm family announced to Skeeter that they wanted to go to a big political demonstration taking place off island the next day. Did Skeeter want to join them? He wasn't so sure that he wanted to come along. He had never participated in a political protest, and he wasn't so sure that he wanted to.

The line from the Rolling Stones song kept coming into his head: "I went down to the demonstration, to get my fair share of abuse." And he was pretty certain that he didn't want his share, fair or not. "I don't know. What's gonna happen, anyway?"

"Just a lot of people are going to go out to the nuclear submarine base and demonstrate against atomic weapons on the subs," Ross told him. "Nothing really heavy. We'll probably just march in a big parade with hundreds of other people. Probably sing songs, while waving signs or carrying banners. Probably hear a speech or two and maybe some good folk songs, have a picnic lunch and then come home. No big deal really. It should be kind of fun, and the nukes really are bad news."

"Really, that's all?" It would get him off the island for a while and away from his troubles here. And Ross said it wouldn't be any big deal. But then again. The idea just seemed kind of stupid to him.. "Nah, I don't think that I'll come with you."

That's when Austin said, "I don't think this is Skeeter's kind of thing, Ross. He's more the whack you in the shin and run for it type, than the 'all we are saying is give peace a chance' type. Best we leave him at home."

"Hey, it is going to be kind of fun," said Carl.

"Yeah, come on along," urged Annie.

Now Skeeter was feeling a little miffed by Austin's comment. Kind of mocking him, and hinting maybe he was a little afraid to join them. Fuck no, man.

"Okay. I don't see the point. You ain't going to change anything with your hippie dippy peace march. But you guys want me to come along. Okay."

The others laughed and Ross slapped him on the back. Austin had what looked like a sly, little grin on her face to Skeeter. But now he thought, what the hell.

So the next morning they piled into Hal's big, old Chevy and headed for the ferry dock at Keystone up by Coupeville that would take them to Port Townsend. There was a slight breeze, but the water was only mildly choppy as the ferry began the forty minute crossing. They all hung out on the upper deck, letting the wind whip their hair about, and soaking up the warm rays of the morning sun.

Skeeter looked at the rust on the aging ferry. It made him wonder if the bolts holding the hull together were getting rusty as well. Oh well, it had served for over fifty years, maybe it was good for another fifty. Even if it did come apart in a storm, he probably wouldn't be on it that day, he hoped.

Skeeter was enjoying himself. He didn't have any weapons on him, but he felt oddly safe in the present company. It made no sense to him. Here he was in a group of pansy ass peaceniks, who couldn't likely fight their way out of any sort of trouble. Something about the mere presence of this small group of young people, however, who seemed to genuinely like him, put him at ease. He tried to sort it out in his mind. They sure as hell didn't "have his back," in the normal sense of that. But he instinctively knew that they wouldn't readily abandon him. There was something comforting in that thought.

Once they had landed at the dock in PT, they parked and went into the Townhouse Tavern located adjacent to the dock and ordered some soup and some beer for lunch. The Townhouse was an old tavern with a long, finely polished wooden bar, and a friendly clientele that reminded Skeeter of his hometown Doghouse Tavern. He was told that patrons who were too out of it to drive home, and weary, low budget travelers could pay a buck and sack out on mattresses laid out in the rooms above the tavern.

He looked out the big front window of the tavern. There was another group of young people like the gang from the farm piling out of a van and coming in for lunch. They too, it turned out, were on their way to the Trident Submarine Base. As they left the tavern and drove down Main Street of Port Townsend, he started noticing others who appeared to be part of the pilgrimage to the base that day. What had he stumbled into when he met the Nature Kids?

With lunch over they continued on to the Hood Canal Bridge and the Kitsap Peninsula, finally arriving by early afternoon at the rally in front of the Naval Base at Bangor on Hood Canal. And what a sight it was for a newcomer to political protest like Skeeter. Hundreds of colorful banners and nearly 4000 people of all ages and descriptions had come that day, May 22, 1977, to protest the presence of the Trident nuclear submarines on Hood Canal.

The organizers had set up headquarters in an old farmhouse near the base. They had been protesting the presence of the submarines here for some time now. Members of their group would leaflet visitors and workers at the entrance to the base, passing along information on issues concerning the work there. A number of them had engaged in acts of civil disobedience, illegally blocking the entrance or entering onto the base, and they had served weeks to months in jail already for their actions.

They did this in order to draw public attention to the craziness of spending tax dollars on the nuclear submarines at the base. Their leaflets pointed out that a Trident submarine carried enough nuclear warheads to destroy up to four hundred cities. That made a Trident submarine captain, an unelected military man, the second most powerful person on earth after the US President. They would roam the sea at depths that made them undetectable, and they were capable of launching their long-range missiles at a moment's notice.

The Soviets now lived with new fear and uncertainty. This kind of fear, as Skeeter knew from first hand experience, could easily lead to irrational behavior. While most Americans believed that the submarines were just a defensive weapon to deter aggression - that their nation was incapable of launching a treacherous, preemptive attack- Skeeter wasn't all that sure.

He had seen the US military use whatever tactics and weapons it deemed necessary in order to defeat its enemies. Napalm, torture, carpet bombing, you name it. There were no such things as honorable rules of war. There were the weaker and there were the stronger, and cunning and treachery were tactics typically employed by both. He had heard it said that truth was the first casualty of war, which made a lot of sense, if you considered that lies and propaganda were just a normal tool in the toolbox of any country at war. Lying to the enemy, and when it was deemed necessary to the war effort, lying to ones own citizens, was the norm.

As he read the pamphlets produced by the demonstration organizers as they prepared to join the march, he began to see the logic of their approach. They also shared his anger at those in power and the system that kept them there. A few months ago he had also imagined that a guerrilla army, not unlike that which had fought the great US military to a standstill in Vietnam, was the key to successful revolt. Now he was not so sure. Violent revolution, often fought in the name of freedom and justice, just as likely seemed to teach people that further violence would also be rewarded. Those who were rewarded for their violence during a revolution easily went on to use violence on a daily basis to remain in power. If the Vietnamese would have likely been better off without US involvement in their civil war, the very fact that they couldn't resolve their internal differences without a war, still meant terrible consequences for the whole society.

After a series of speeches by the protest organizers, demonstrators were invited to join them in an act of civil disobedience, and suddenly people all around them began climbing over the low, barbed wire fence that surrounded the base and pouring onto the grounds. Hundreds of people appeared to be swarming over the fences. Skeeter had never seen anything like it.

"Let's do it," said Austin. And the others nodded their assent. Skeeter was nervous. This was crazy. He knew the power of the US military. They were all going to get themselves beaten all to hell and maybe worse. Were they nuts? You don't mess with the military. But the others were determined to join in the action, and he couldn't get himself to abandon his naive friends. So he started toward the fence with the rest of them, and he tried not to look like he was on his way to the gallows, though that's how he felt. They held hands as they walked across the open field toward the base itself after climbing over the four foot high fence that marked the perimeter.

Skeeter had learned enough by now to know that there was a long, proud tradition of political protest in his native land. He tried to keep reminding himself of the words of Henry David Thoreau on the subject, to keep his courage up: "If the machine of government is of such a nature that it requires you to be the agent of injustice to another, then, I say, break the law."

He could tell that the others were also nervous, but they also felt a safety in numbers. As they looked about them they could see some three hundred others who had also answered the call. A small army of soldiers against war and the preparation for war. And now they were singing, "Gonna lay down my sword and shield, down by the riverside, down by the riverside, down by the riverside. I ain't gonna study war no more, I ain't gonna study war no more..."

The words caught a bit in Skeeter's throat. What a wonderful dream, and here were hundreds of people determined to act on that dream together. And here he was among them. 'If I die today, I will die happy,' he said to himself. At this moment he felt as if he had somehow managed to step out of his petty, foolish day to day self, the one that muddled along rather aimlessly and could so easily meet a pointless death of his own making or orchestrated by others as foolish. As foolish and naive as the present action appeared, it made a lot more sense than what he had been doing up to until now.

Those who had swarmed over the barbed wire onto the base were almost immediately arrested by the Military Police, who began handcuffing them with plastic cuffs and loading them on to waiting buses.

The group from the farm stayed together as they were cuffed for transport on a bus.

Skeeter felt a sudden sinking of his spirits as he felt that familiar moment of helplessness at the hands of government authorities. He had felt it often enough as a GI or as an arrestee by civilian cops. But as they were being herded onto the bus, the driver made some comment about "moving on back." This prompted someone on the bus to begin singing "the driver of the bus says move on back, move on back, move on back, all through the town." Soon everyone on the bus was singing along on the familiar children's song. It immediately relieved much of the tension.

Once they were in the auditorium the several hundred protesters were slowly processed for eventual booking. The authorities realized that this was going to take many hours to accomplish, and it was also obvious that this crowd was no threat to the MPs. So they took off their handcuffs and let them roam freely about the big gymnasium where they were being housed. Eventually they were all served box lunches as well.

To pass the time they sang songs and danced together. Skeeter had expected something altogether different. He had been told about the harsh detention of smaller groups of protestors who had entered the base on previous occasions. But the authorities really were at a loss that day when it came to dealing with so many people. They seemed reluctant to behave in any heavy-handed manner. It was as if they sensed that the crowd that they had under arrest was out to make a public statement, and they were in a somewhat cheerful, even festive mood. Why on earth would the authorities want to spoil that mood, if it made these people easier to manage in mass arrest?

The idealistic crowd of people he was with that day seemed to embody the peace and love that was such a favorite fantasy at the heart of the anti-war movement that had grown up in the 1960's. It was a diverse crowd of flower children, anarchists, Buddhists, Christian believers of various stripes from radical Catholic activists to traditional pacifist Mennonites and Quakers, and there were both the old and the young. And there in a nearby group sat Peter. Did he see him? What did it matter? Joanne was also with that group of protesters. She saw Skeeter, and she gave him a wink. He made his first contacts that afternoon with the group, Veterans for Peace.

The group of them swayed as the music of their combined voices echoed off the walls and ceiling of the gymnasium. It didn't feel real to him, this moment. It was dream-like. And so far removed from the moment he had smashed Jack's leg with the tire iron, or the moment when a mortar round landed in the back of the transport truck he was riding on in Vietnam. This was not Skeeter's world.

Later that day they were all transported to a jail in Tacoma, and that evening, those who were first-time offenders at the Trident base were released and given letters barring their reentry to the base. A dozen or so others who had already received letters from a previous arrest at the base were held in jail.

This caused a stir among those who had been released. "This is no good. We can't let them make an example of our brothers and sisters," one of the leaders of the action called out.

Skeeter had hoped that their release might mean that they could return to the island now. But, no. The consensus among the group was that they had to return to the base and get arrested a second time, in solidarity with those still being held.

He thought, maybe, they were pushing their luck. The MPs weren't the sweethearts some of these folks wanted to believe. They could start cracking heads if they pissed them off enough. He spent an anxious night alongside the others, camped out by the old farmhouse that was home base for the Ground Zero crowd.

Skeeter was not at all happy about returning to the base and climbing over the fence the next morning. But he did it, and he kept his fears to himself. Much to his relief they were treated much as they had been the day before, and the solidarity among them did eventually allow everyone who had been arrested and held over night to also get off with only a warning or minor punishment for the repeat offenders.

"I am so glad we got out of that without getting our heads cracked," Skeeter confided to Austin, on the ferry on their way back to the island.

"Yeah," she said. "It could have gone a lot worse. There are two Catholic priests, Philip and Daniel Berrigan, who received stiff prison sentences for anti nuke actions. Kind of heroic, but I know I'm not that tough or brave."

Was this all a wasted effort? He wondered. What had they really accomplished? Those priests she mentioned. Maybe courageous martyrs in a righteous cause, but who could know if their actions would lead to some positive result?

When they finally arrived back home a day later, they were all feeling buoyed up by the experience. The daily drudge work and the petty quarrels among them seemed like nothing more than passing squalls. Skeeter felt like he had had a taste of the peaceable kingdom here on earth. Was it no more than a fleeting, implausible dream? There was this thing with Jack that still hung over him, and the GJB crowd didn't seem like they were looking for him just so that they could all have a good chat.

Chapter Twelve

It was sometime later that week that Austin noticed the flea bites on Skeeter's bare ankles when they were all loafing around the house one afternoon. "Seems like your dog could use a good bath and some flea powder, don't you think?" She asked. About then Rat Dog scratched at himself and then dug with his teeth at a flea on one of his hind legs.

"Yeah, I suppose so," replied Skeeter. "You wanna help?" He asked.

"Sure," she said.

"Okay. How about now."

"Okay." And they went off together to the utility room to prepare a bath for Rat Dog. They found a big wash tub on the porch that they filled with warm water. Then the two of them coaxed the reluctant dog into the basin and started washing him down with rag cloths. He seemed to accept it all with a certain stoic resignation. Not his idea of a good time, but he was generally amenable to the suggestions of his human pack members. They then rinsed him and dried him off with a towel and took him out to Skeeter's shed to dry out a bit more before they worked some flea powder into his fur.

It was the first time that the two of them had gone off on their own to do anything, and the first time Austin had been back to the shed since bringing Skeeter here when he arrived. They sat on the floor at the foot of Skeeter's bed, just resting up a bit. He couldn't help but study her a bit, albeit somewhat furtively. She was somewhat slim and athletic, to his eye. And without thinking much about it he blurted: "You're pretty strong for a girl." Then, he hesitated, thinking how odd that must sound, and said: "I mean, you can keep up with the boys when we're working outside on something."

At first she just looked at him as if he were just too strange. Then, she got a big, wide grin on her face, and burst into laughter.

"What's so funny?" He asked, a bit of alarm in his voice, at the thought that she was laughing at him.

She seemed to sense this, as she grabbed his arm and said, "you wanna wrestle? See who is stronger? Think you can pin me?"

It seemed a little odd to wrestle with a girl, but he didn't want her to think he was afraid of the challenge. They were almost the same height, though he had a few pounds on her, and he thought he had some extra muscle besides. He was actually beginning to get a little curious to see how strong she was.

They locked their arms into a wrestling pose and tumbled together to the floor, each trying to roll the other onto their back. He was startled at just how strong she proved to be. He was forced to really exert himself to keep from being toppled over. She was grinning the whole time, but he was beginning to realize that this wasn't going to be some sort of gentle, lovey kind of game. And it sure wasn't sexual.

It was a fair bit of sport, however, with neither of them exerting any kind of brute force. They just twisted and turned and toppled around the room, trying to gain some sort of advantage over the other. He grew anxious a couple of times when it looked like she might just get him flipped on his back. At such times, he really did wrestle all out to prevent that. Rat Dog seemed to be getting caught up in their rivalry as well, and he was barking at them from a safe distance off in the far corner of the room.

Eventually after about fifteen minutes of this, Skeeter did manage to get her over onto her back, and she relaxed and gave him a little nod of agreement that he had bested her in a fair fight. He was a bit relieved to have won, and just a little unsure that maybe she hadn't really wanted to win. But then again, he did think that he had somewhat of an edge over her in the muscle department. In any case, it wasn't as much of an edge as he had thought going into this.

He lay on top of her momentarily, each of them panting a bit, staring into each others eyes, and beginning to realize that another emotion was taking over. He wasn't sure of what to make of it, so he began to slowly roll off of her, a move that she then resisted. That was when they began to tentatively plant small kisses on each others lips.

Their match may not have seemed like foreplay at the time, but it now seemed to easily lead into a sexual tryst that Skeeter would not soon forget. Perhaps the extended drought in his romantic life contributed to this feeling, but there was definitely something special about their coupling that day. And the ice was certainly broken between them for more of the same in the future. He had sensed for some time that she was unattached and somewhat available, but he wasn't really at all confident that she saw much of anything in him.

There was one slightly troubling moment when Austin noticed the long scar on Skeeter's thigh, and as she passed her fingers over it, she asked, "what's this?"

A momentary frown appeared on Skeeter's face before he reluctantly muttered, "Just an old injury... from Nam."

At that her eyes widened and she looked at him more directly now. As if asking, who was this guy? "So how did it happen," she asked.

He refused to meet her eyes as he said, "Nothing much to tell. Nothing heroic, that's for sure, just a little bad luck."

She didn't press him for more. And he appeared visibly relieved at that. She stayed with him that night and nights to follow. And when she cradled him in her arms, he soon fell asleep and sometimes even slept 'til dawn. And if he awoke in the middle of the night from some terrible nightmare, she was often there to hold him and soothe the trembling.

He was ashamed of this. His weakness exposed. But there was nothing he could do about it. He sometimes thought it would be better to just drive her away, like he had Shelley, so long ago. So that there would be no witnesses to his shame. But he didn't.

The days passed and Skeeter fell into a daily routine of activities, work and play on the farm, that now also included visits to their "shedroom" by Austin. He only made rare forays out into the world, and he preferred those to be after dark, such as a moonlight walk on the beach at Double Bluff or maybe a day trip in the car with others to some destination not part of his old haunts.

One sunny afternoon as he and Austin and Rat Dog lay basking in the green grass of the upper meadow, she asked him, "Do you miss your little cabin at all?"

He thought about it. Yes. Sure, he hadn't been the happiest camper in the park, but there were things he did like about his life in that small cabin back in the deep woods. Others might regard him with a certain amount of contempt, just a scruffy, young guy with little to call his own, and little prospect of ever earning much in order to have anything. A backwoods bum, living in a little shack. But he had liked it. He had liked his freedom. He had enjoyed waking up to the sound of bird song and just listening to the wind whispering in the tall tree tops. And the air. You couldn't beat the sweet smell of the forest air. It made you want to take a deep breath, just fill your lungs and slowly let it go.

He was reminded of a poem his mother was fond of by the great Irish poet William Butler Yeats. "I will rise and go now, and go to Innisfree..." The poem begins and then continues to tell of the poet's plan to build a little cottage on the shore of the Lake Isle of Innisfree. And how he would have a garden with "nine bean rows." And the poem eventually concludes with a line which says something like: "and I will find some peace there, for peace comes dropping slow." Yes, that's what Skeeter had sought out in his retreat in the deep woods.

His time on the farm had made him aware of some of what had been missing from his life in the woods, but he still had to admit that there was much that was good there. "Yes, I miss my cabin sometimes," he finally answered. He shuddered to think what a mess Jack might have made of it by now. "I felt free there."

Austin leaned her head onto his lap as she stroked Rat Dog. "Among the nicest times of my childhood were the trips to the cabin that my dad and his friends built for deer hunting. We kids loved those trips. The long drive in the car, even if we had to dodge my father's hand swiped across the back seat to try and swat us little brats, or at least threaten that he might connect next time, if we didn't behave," she laughed.

"We always got to the deep woods long after dark," she continued. "If we had been asleep, we would always wake up to watch for deer. It was always magical to me. The only sound would be the drone of the car engine. And the head lights would shine on the single lane dirt road, not much more than a trail with grass growing between the wheel ruts."

He looked over at her now and noticed the way the sunlight made her reddish hair almost gold. Was she pretty, in some conventional ways our society defined that? He had no idea. She sure didn't seem too concerned about that, in any case. No make up, or adornment of any kind. Especially when she smiled though, she was as pretty as any picture he had ever seen.

"Almost always," she continued, "we would catch sight of a bright star-like reflection of a deer's eye somewhere on the road to the cabin.

Most of the time we would only get the tiniest glimpse of a brown form fleeing into the dark forest."

He continued to study her. Was this what made someone truly attractive? Not strutting around like a peacock. Not putting on some pose to attract attention, but genuine, authentic enthusiasm for a wondrous world outside of oneself. That was what was appealing, her sharing her delight in beautiful things outside of herself. What made anyone potentially interesting and attractive? Not beauty aids, it seemed. Nor things intended purely to impress.

Her eyes had a dreamy, far away look to them now, as she continued her story. "Those trips to the woods with our parents had a lasting effect on us kids. Probably the strongest proof of this is the fact that I am here today living on this old farm on the edge of another forest out here in the Pacific Northwest."

"Do you ever miss your home, or your family back there?" He asked.

She seemed to think about that before she answered. "I miss my family sometimes. And sometimes I miss the scent of the old pine woods back home. I grew up mostly in the city, but my time spent in the country gave me some of my fondest memories of people sharing those places with me."

She peered into his eyes as she spoke, as if to say, listen, this is no idle chatter. "The world of the wild has always been a wondrous place for me, and a perfect medium of exchange in life, the shared pleasure."

Now he studied her more carefully than he ever had before. She seemed to utterly defy his previous notions of romantic love. All of those silly love songs, that had no more or less meaning than the lovely mating songs of the birds, gave one strange notions of love. He had a hunch that she might likely never utter the words, "I love you," or ask to get "engaged." With someone like her, you were engaged in the shared pleasure of this beautiful, amazing world, and if you weren't, then spending further time with you would be of no further interest to her.

A peculiar thing had happened to him. He had been of little interest to her or anyone else, unless you included Jack, when he was constantly meditating on how the world had double crossed him and dealt him some dirty blows. But when he had begun to share the little pleasures of a pancake breakfast or a walk in the woods, or planting a garden, or joining in a march for peace, he had slowly been transformed in the eyes of others and even in his own eyes.

He had no clear idea how the intimate, sexual kind of shared pleasure was any different than the other pleasures he shared with people. He had some inklings. The fact that it was so tied to procreation of human life made it somehow qualitatively different. But he hadn't been able to sort it out much beyond that. It did occur to him that this was the stuff of powerful attachment. And that scared him a bit. As the folk poet sang: "If you got nothin', you got nothin' to lose." Undoubtedly, this new state of being meant some loss of freedom, but then again, something to lose, meant you had something, didn't it.

....

As Skeeter sat on his bed one evening, mending a tear in one of the used shirts he had bought awhile back at Good Cheer, the second hand store in Langley, Austin came in and announced to him, "I'm leaving on a trip tomorrow. I have some dear, old friends I want to visit down in California. I know you would love them, Skeeter. I hope someday soon you'll get to meet them too."

Skeeter wasn't so sure about that. Why did she need to see them, anyway? Wasn't he and their little family here on the farm enough for her? What did these old friends mean to her anyway?

She told him, "I'll catch the Evergreen Trailways bus from Freeland tomorrow. It'll take me into Seattle, where I can catch a train for San Francisco."

It was all too abrupt a change for Skeeter. They had never really discussed a life either of them had outside of the little circle on the farm. It had never occurred to him until now that there were others, that it occurred to him now, quite likely included lovers from the past, waiting for her some where. Until now, she had never mentioned a circle of friends elsewhere that she had certainly known longer and maybe felt closer to than she did him. Of course, there was family elsewhere, the younger brother and sister and the parents and grandparents she had occasionally mentioned in passing. But he had never really asked her much about her past, and he never talked that much about his own life, as if there really was much of anything to tell anyway.

But now, with her announcement that she wanted to go see some "dear friends" elsewhere, he felt a whole sea of conflicting emotions rolling and tumbling inside of him. And this included doubts about the idea of coming with her someday to meet them. Did he really want to be introduced to her friends? And he wasn't so sure that he would be all that comfortable around them. Probably college educated, city bred, nice enough people, but what would they really think of him?

"I'll drive you down to the Mukilteo Ferry dock. You can catch the bus on the mainland side," he said, but without much enthusiasm. They had a somewhat uneasy evening together. And almost as a way to ease his sense of loss of her, he was distancing himself emotionally from her, slow to touch her or show much affection. And he would try to change the subject whenever she tried to tell him about her plans for the trip.

Finally as they prepared to ease into bed, she exploded at him. "What is this bullshit? I plan to go off on a visit to friends and you get all sulky on me."

"We'll, we haven't really known each other very long, you know," he said.

"We're lovers!" She shouted at him. "Something that is something."

"Yeah well, it's one thing to go rolling around the sheets with someone, but it doesn't really necessarily mean you are all that tight with each other."

Now her eyes were blazing. "No, that's true. Sometimes maybe it don't mean shit."

He hadn't heard her swear in all the time he'd known her. Maybe he really didn't know her all that well.

"Yeah, maybe..." He muttered.

"I know that you like to keep your cool. Why, you've never once said anything to make me think there is anything special about us together. And you won't even give your dog a real name. What is it? If he had a name would it mean that you might be more attached to him, might even miss him if something happened to him?"

"Maybe..." He mumbled, not liking where this was going.

"I think I'm going to spend the night in the house with the others."

"Suit yourself," he said, already feeling a kind of sinking feeling, and a dull ache just beginning in his gut as she strode off into the night.

Austin left in the morning and Skeeter stayed cool. All sorts of conflicting thoughts and emotions swam around in him. One minute he caught himself saying to himself: 'Time to move on. What do I really know about her? Seems like she might be kind of a slut, sleeping around. Just happened I was the most available guy around here.' The next minute he was thinking: 'She's the best thing that ever happened to me. What kind of an idiot would I be not to do everything I can to keep her?' But in the end, he remained "cool." And she left after breakfast with no special moment given or received between them.

. . . .

Skeeter started having nightmares again. He would wake up in a sweat after some dream in which he was being chased by armed assassins. Sometimes it was Jack, other times it looked like people from the armed revolutionary cell in Seattle.

The very worst of these dreams came one early morning. He dreamed that he was one of the soldiers in a unit, maybe Lieutenant Calley's at My Lai, ordered to turn his gun on a ditch filled with crying women and children. He didn't want to pull the trigger on his semi automatic rifle. He kept begging the lieutenant to let him go do some other job. Let someone else do this. But no. It was an order, and others were already firing their guns into the ditch filled with people.

He thought about the consequences of not pulling the trigger. He thought about what could happen. And at My Lai the army had originally covered up the whole incident, praising those involved and reprimanding some who had tried to stop the massacre. There was a helicopter pilot who had seen what was going on and had landed, and he and his men had tried to stop the killing. They couldn't bring themselves to fire on their own, and eventually they had gathered up some of the endangered villagers and flown away. When the pilot later reported what had happened, he was reprimanded. Only much later, when a nosy peacenik reporter wouldn't let go of the story, did the truth come out, and eventually Calley received a little jail time.

No, Skeeter definitely would be better off if he pulled the trigger on the women and children in the ditch. He would be arrested if he didn't, or the lieutenant or one of the others might decide to execute him right there on the spot for his insubordination. He kept begging to be let go, but the lieutenant was insistent. It was an order. Did he intend to disobey orders? Was he ready to face the consequences? Was he a traitor to his own? Or worse yet, a weakling and a coward, not strong enough or tough enough to do the dirty work required in this situation?

He began to cry out. "I can't do it!" His rifle fell from his hands and he fell to the ground and curled up into a ball, wailing like a little child. When he awoke he was trembling and covered with sweat. After he had had some time to recover and reflect on what had happened, he decided that there was something he had to do. That morning he went into town to pay a visit to the bookstore and Peter again.

He arrived around noon at the store. There was a lot of activity going on in the backroom of the store. People were coming and going. Leaflets were being sorted and folded for distribution. Peter was obviously preoccupied with the work at hand, but when he saw him, he nodded to Skeeter and looked for an opportune moment for them to duck outside to talk.

They walked a little way down the alley across the street from the store and leaned against a brick wall. Peter looked kind of pissed, but Skeeter wasn't sure if it was directed at him. Then he lit a cigarette and started smoking, and when Skeeter turned to face him, Peter blew some smoke right into his face. Okay, that answers that question, he said to himself. "So what's going on around here?" asked Skeeter.

"You don't know? One of our comrades was killed recently planting a pipe bomb at a grocery store in solidarity with a boycott. Now the pigs have started a grand jury investigation, and they are arresting those they consider the most vulnerable of our comrades. Three women are already in jail for refusing to cooperate with the grand jury. Women with children are their first target, assuming that such women will betray their comrades most readily in order to avoid long term separation from their families."

Then he gave Skeeter a cold, hard stare as he said, "What they don't seem to understand is that our women comrades can be tough and loyal. Those of us who have not been jailed are busy organizing demonstrations of solidarity with our jailed comrades." He paused momentarily to glare at Skeeter, and then asked, "So what do you want here, anyway?"

Fair enough, thought Skeeter. "I just wanted to let you know that I heard that your friends at the safe house were out on the island asking after me. Tell them for me that I'm no threat to them. I won't be telling anyone anything I know about them."

"And why exactly should they trust you?"

Skeeter didn't have an answer to that. He just looked kind of hang dog. There was something about disappointing Peter, even now, that felt awful. He had so admired the man's intellect and his passion for justice. But he knew instinctively that he had done the right thing when he had ditched the gang in the Seattle safe house. But he didn't know how to explain all that to Peter. He just looked like one more chicken-shit little guy to him, ready to cringe and obey rather than fight for a better world.

He returned to the island with no real sense of anything resolved. So much seemed confusing to him. He could understand loyalty to comrades in common cause, but he was less sure about what constituted a just cause to devote oneself to. He had read a quote somewhere attributed to Che Guevarra, "At the risk of seeming ridiculous, let me say that the true revolutionary is guided by great feelings of love."

He could get behind that. But what if it was reckless, careless love? False or shallow love? Misguided or blind? As much as he was attached to Rat Dog, for instance, he didn't totally admire Rat Dog's almost absolute loving devotion to him. He could be a mass murderer and Rat Dog would probably still follow him around devotedly, so long as he displayed the proper alpha male behavior.

………

Not long after, he was lying in bed absorbed in a new book. *One Straw Revolution* by a Japanese farmer named Masanobu Fukuoka. The author was challenging some of the most basic assumptions of agriculture. It seemed like Skeeter was slowly getting an education that had so far eluded him. This book was a good segue from his previous read, a book by a brainy American farmer, *The Unsettling of America* by Wendell Berry. Until now, Skeeter had never thought of how books could be windows or doors into worlds and ideas not otherwise easily accessible to him.

His calm absorption was tinged with a sense of anticipation. Austin could burst through that door at any moment. She wouldn't stay in California forever. She could be on her way back right now, and Skeeter and Rat Dog were waiting for her return in a state of alert anticipation. Reconciliation shouldn't be all that hard. He was already working out the apology that he would offer her.

The silence was suddenly shattered by a rifle blast that tore a hole in the shed about a foot from his head. Skeeter immediately snuffed out the candle and searched frantically under his mattress for the pistol. But it proved unnecessary. There was no further gunfire, and after a momentary silence he could hear a truck engine revving up and then the sound of the motor slowly receding, until it could no longer be heard. It took another minute for Skeeter's racing heart to return to normal.

Ross stuck his head out the back door and called out: "Hey, man, you okay out there?"

"Yeah," shouted Skeeter.

That was when Skeeter spotted Rat Dog, lying in a pool of blood near the shed door. The calm that had almost returned to the evening farm was once again shattered by Skeeter's scream. "No!" The little dog was whimpering softly, so he was still alive, but he couldn't seem to rise from where he lay.

Skeeter approached the little bundle of black hair, curled up in a ball, beginning to tremble. Was he going into shock? He gently picked up the small, limp form and wrapped him in a blanket. How he wanted to kill the son of a bitch who had done this. But he knew that he had to deal with Rat Dog first.

He asked Ross to call the vet and tell him to meet Skeeter at the clinic, as he gathered Rat Dog and hurried out the door. "I've got to get him to the doc" he announced to the crowd now gathered around them.

It took about ten minutes to get his dog over to the clinic at the corner of Cultus Bay Road and the highway. He drove as fast as he dared, with one hand on the wheel and the other caressing Rat Dog, lying on the seat next to him.

When they arrived at the clinic, there was the new veterinarian, a big, blond Scandinavian looking guy who was all business, standing waiting for them.

"Thanks, for dropping everything and coming out for this," Skeeter mumbled out the open truck window, as he pulled up alongside the vet. The doc immediately circled the truck, without a word, and opened the passenger door and began examining the little dog. He opened the dog's mouth and examined his gums. "Not too bad," he said. "Still a lot of pink," suggesting that the dog's circulation was still pretty good.

After a quick inspection, he told Skeeter, "Pick him up as gently as you can and bring him in." Then he led Skeeter with the dog to the entrance. He unlocked the door and ushered them back into a lab room, where he immediately began work on the dog.

"What's the name of your pup?" He asked as he worked.

Skeeter was embarrassed to say Rat Dog. Instead, he muttered in a low, raspy voice, "Buddy."

"And what the heck happened?"

"Accident with a gun," he mumbled.

The vet gave him a slightly disgusted look, then returned his attention to the dog. "Well, Buddy here looks like he is gonna need an IV. He's lost some blood." Then he pointed to a place on his leg. "The bullet entered and exited here, in his leg," the vet explained as he showed Skeeter the bloody wound.

Skeeter felt sick. It was one thing to risk his own neck, but look what his actions had cost his dog. And it could have been one of the folks at the farm, caught in a cross-fire. Who knows? "So what are his chances?" Skeeter croaked.

"I'm not sure. At least the bullet passed through and didn't appear to hit a major artery or a bone. But with the blood loss and the risk of infection... Let me get the liquid drip going, and I'll cover the wound after cleaning it out good. Then an antibiotic and we'll just have to wait and see how he does. Leave him here with me now. You can come back in the morning."

Skeeter hesitated. He didn't want to leave the dog's side. Then he thought for a moment and said, "okay, I'll be back in the morning."

He kissed the dog on the head and hurried out to the truck. He ground the gears in his rush to be out of there. Then the truck roared as he raced the engine and the tires screeched as he burned rubber crossing the highway onto Langley Road, heading into town. As he drove at break neck speed toward town, he kept fingering the trigger of the pistol.

He hit the brakes as he approached the city limits, and drove the rest of the way to The Doghouse at a normal speed. He looked for Jack's truck as he slowly drove by. No sign of it. He circled the block, cruising up Second Street, still no truck. Where was the bastard?

Had he gone home? Skeeter now drove a bit more cautiously, but with a calm and focus on every detail of the task at hand. It took him about ten minutes to reach Jack's place, just off East Harbor Road, on Brainer Road. Set back from the road down a two hundred foot driveway bordered by thick, twenty foot tall hemlocks and firs. He pulled off the road just past the driveway, and nudged the truck into a narrow trail left over from some previous logging operation in the area years ago. Once he knew the truck was well hidden, he cut the engine and pulled the shotgun out from behind the seat. He pulled the shell of bird shot out of the chamber and replaced it with a rifled slug. Then he cautiously started making his way through the thick brush toward where he knew the house to be.

There was a sliver of moon casting a little light through a high, thin cloud cover that allowed him to more or less see where he was going in the dark. Still, an occasional branch would tear at his clothes and the thorns of the salmonberry bushes scraped his wrists and caught him in the cheek and occasionally grazed his forehead as he walked.

The gun felt light, gripped in his right hand, as he made his way toward the house. Once he was close enough to see the nightlight that glowed from the front porch, illuminating a cleared area out front of the house, he stopped and crouched down, resting on one knee and studying the scene through the foliage.

It never once entered Skeeter's mind to call the police on Jack. Maybe that's what city folks of the right pedigree did, but no one in his experience expected the police to rescue them from much of anything. If you lived out in the country like his people did, you weren't very likely to get help from the cops when you needed them anyway. There were people who tried to convince him that the police were public servants, out to protect and serve the public. His own experience was very mixed on that subject. Yeah, some of the local guys were alright, but others he knew chose law enforcement because they were just school bullies who had moved on to bigger and better prey. He thought the line in the old Bob Dylan song: "The cops don't need you, and buddy they expect the same," pretty much said it. That was why he sat out there in the woods near Jack's house on this dark night by himself, without a second thought.

Not much really to see. No truck. No sign of any activity. He knew Jack lived alone. Who the hell would want to live with the son of a bitch? But he was smart enough not to be here right now. Or had Jack done it? After all, he had just been to town and he was nowhere to be found. But Jack had been alerted to his possible presence on the farm when he had seen Rat Dog with Austin a while back. The gang from Seattle may have also figured out that he was out at the farm as well. But that seemed unlikely. No, it was definitely Jack. Then he heard a car engine, and he could see headlights as a truck made its way down the drive, with little or no sense of caution. So, not so smart after all.

The truck parked in front of the house. Jack got out. He hardly looked around as he made his way toward the door. What was it with this guy? Did he want to die? Or what? No fear of the consequences of his actions. You'd think that he had just been out for a leisurely drive. Maybe, as such a predator, he couldn't imagine that anyone would stalk him. Even a guy he had just tried to kill. Well, maybe he hadn't particularly tried too hard to kill him. Maybe just shot at the biggest part of the shed from a long distance. Didn't really think about what it would do. Just knew that Skeeter would get the message that Jack knew where he was and could get him anytime he felt like it.

What he, no doubt, hadn't counted on was that a truly pissed and deadly serious Skeeter would come looking for him. And now he had him in his sights. Funny how people put up bright lights around their houses thinking that it warded off danger. When, in fact, it mostly lit up the occupants for an intruder hidden in the dark, and it made approach even easier, because you didn't even need to carry your own light, which would have been easy to spot anyway, if the surrounds were completely dark. But, in the mistaken belief that it made them safer, whole cities full of people had made their night time towns almost as bright as day.

It was probably just stupid, irrational fear of the dark, as much as anything. Although it denied them the pleasure of the grand night sky, and it used a hell of a lot of electricity in the process. If even half of all those lights were turned off at night in cities around the world, there would hardly be a need for all those coal burning power plants, dams or nuclear power plants.

Skeeter held the shotgun to his shoulder. He was breathing normally as he searched along the barrel to line up the bead at the end of it with Jack's ugly form. He found him and slid his finger into place on the trigger. He wanted so badly to squeeze the trigger. But a torrent of conflicting thoughts and emotions flooded through his head. Austin might be back any day now, and he longed for their reunion. He didn't want to abandon his dog that eagerly awaited his return at the vet's office. And why should he let Jack's death earn him a lifetime behind bars, locked away from all he loved in this life. But it took every ounce of his willpower to resist the urge to pull the trigger. So much hung in the balance at that moment. Rage battled with reason inside him. "Bang, you're dead," he whispered to himself, then stood up and slowly backed out of the brush, making his way back to the truck.

Chapter Thirteen

"Hey, man," Ross said. "I really wish I could have done something, but the others made it a rule, no guns here. They just pretended not to notice in your case."

"That's okay. Thanks for wanting to do something, but it isn't your fight. I fucked up. And I understand completely that I had better move on."

"But where?"

"I think I'll just go back to my old place."

"He'll find you there."

"Yeah, probably..."

"We'll miss you, man," said Ross.

"We'll be thinking of you whenever we eat some of those peas in the garden," said Carl.

"Thanks," Skeeter said as he hugged all around. No hesitation with the gay boys on his part now. They were just part of the untypical, intentional little family he had been part of at the farm for the past few months. Then he went out and gathered everything into the old truck and headed for home.

After a stop at the store for some supplies, he made his way out to the little cabin out in the big woods south of Greenbank. Nothing much had changed out there. Jack hadn't punched anymore holes through windows, and mice, fortunately, hadn't made too much of a mess. The absence of food seemed to have reduced their interest in the place.

After spending some time cleaning and setting things in order, Skeeter sat down to some lunch. Then he and Rat Dog, who was now on the mend, went for a walk. Fortunately, he seemed to have had a clean wound after it bled out, where the bullet had passed through his rear leg. They sat together on the soft cushion of hemlock needles in the partial shade of a tree.

It seemed that he was back where he started. Is that all life is? A series of circlings around that bring you right back to where you began your journey? Had anything changed? He abandoned the effort to answer that question. He stepped back into the present and opened a book that had captured his interest a while back and read the opening lines again:

"I went to the woods because I wished to live deliberately, to front only the essential facts of life, and see if I could not learn what it had to teach, and not, when I came to die, discover that I had not lived."

He spent the rest of that afternoon absorbed in the reading of Henry David Thoreau's *Walden Pond.* He tried to figure out how to come to terms with his own enforced version of going to the woods. He had moved here from his parent's house over a year ago just to escape people and the demands of people. He'd had mixed results. There were times when he'd enjoyed the woods, the proximity of a wild nature that didn't threaten him the way so much of human society did. In fact, he had found a certain amount of peace here. But he had also discovered, upon meeting up with the Nature Kids, that there was more to life.

He fell into a daily routine of work in his own small garden. He also hunted and fished a bit. He went over to his folks' place and visited once in a while, and after one visit he brought back three laying hens and built them a small coop near the cabin. He avoided Langley and the Doghouse. He didn't seem to need a steady supply of beer anymore. He had even begun to drink herbal teas that they had introduced him to at the farm.

Nearly a month passed with little of real consequence happening. Was Jack just biding his time, he wondered? Skeeter seemed to still be living in a state of low level terror, always wondering if Jack might do something more.

Is this how police states kept people in line, he wondered? Stalin and the Shah of Iran and others like them apparently liked to have secret police keep the populace in a state of daily fear. It was enough to simply grab some innocent citizen at random off the street and subject them to hellish torture for a time, and then release them back into the populace to tell their tale of woe to whoever would listen. People generally got the message. No one was safe. Resistance would be futile. So all people could do was just cringe and obey.

And Skeeter? He still carried his pistol with him when he went out, and at home he liked to have the shotgun close at hand. There were times when fear would take hold of him. Moments in the pitch, black night, when he would tremble in the dark, and then be seized by a terrible sense of shame and humiliation at the realization that Jack was getting what he wanted. "The coward dies a thousand deaths, the brave man only once."

He had thought there for a while that things had changed in his life, but now as he looked around him, it didn't look like much had changed at all. At such times the impulse to hunt down Jack and end this thing once and for all in a Western cowboy style shoot out was almost overwhelming. At other times he thought, no, he didn't need to play at all fair with Jack. He should use his hunting skills to stalk Jack like you would any dangerous predator and make sure that he got the drop on the bastard and shot straight from some hidden vantage point. That was the way to end this. And then become the prime suspect in murder? Discover a new kind of fear, that of the fugitive from the law, always having to look over his shoulder for the lawman sent to bring him in? And then what? The hellish life dished out in prison, for who knows how many god awful years? No good alternatives seemed to exist.

So he just lived day to day, afraid too much of the time. Yet, he could be content at other times, when he and his dog would take long walks out into the sanctuary of the deep woods, where they would spend hours in wild nature's embrace. Most recently he had come across another writer whose words found a responsive chord in Skeeter's own being:

"I know that tomorrow or next year or in twenty years
I shall not see these things - and it does not matter,
It does not hurt;
They will be here. And when the whole human race
Has been like me rubbed out, they will still be here:
Storms, moon and ocean,
Dawn and the birds. And I say this: their beauty has
more meaning
Than the whole human race and the race of birds."

Was it misanthropic? Sometimes he thought so, as he read these words penned by the nature worshipping poet, Robinson Jeffers. But mostly, it didn't matter to him. The poet's words seemed to ring true for him, and they were a source of a certain comfort to him.

A day came when he couldn't resist the temptation to check in with his old friends over at the farm. It seemed to go well enough at first. Everyone greeted him warmly and they wanted to know what he'd been up to. He smiled and offered a little of his news, but all along he kept looking distractedly over shoulder and all around him, expecting any moment that Austin would appear, to greet him as well.

It was obvious to everyone, what was going on. Finally Ross just blurted it out, "Austin only came back long enough to gather her stuff and then she headed back down to California."

Skeeter didn't know what to say. So she really had found something down there more attractive than what she had up here. Skeeter tried to act as if it was no big deal, but he wasn't fooling anybody. He hugged them all around and promised to come by again soon.

When he was back in the truck he started to feel the aching in his gut. The news of her departure and the fact that she had never made any effort to see him again was beginning to sink in. He made a sudden u turn on Bush Point Road and ten minutes later he was parked in front of the Doghouse.

He didn't give a damn. Nothing mattered much. "When you got nothin', you got nothin' to lose," kept running through his head. He wanted to get real drunk that night, but once he was settled on a stool at the bar he discovered that the beer didn't taste that good. It seemed to leave an unpleasant acid taste in his throat and stomach. He thought he might just puke it all up if he kept drinking. So he just paid his bill and left.

He didn't sleep with the shotgun that night, nor any night thereafter. "Nothin' to lose..." It seemed. For a while nothing had any flavor to it, and the colors of the world, the summer blooms, the red berries, the blue skies filled with cumulus clouds, nothing seemed worthy of his attention anymore. But as the days passed some little glimmer of desire began to grow in him again. He began wondering if he might someday again meet up with Austin. 'The best thing that had ever happened to me, getting close to her.' He thought. But he hadn't been able to keep her in his life.

He went back into Seattle one day to do some shopping and while he was there he decided to visit the bookstore. Peter was there. At first he ignored Skeeter. Then when it was clear that he was just there to buy some books, he just treated him like any other customer. Took his order, searched the inventory and brought him several books on Skeeter's list.

As he took Skeeter's money, he murmured. "I don't know if it's so wise for you to come around here. I don't know what the people I introduced you to might decide to do to you. That is your problem."

Skeeter just looked him in the eye for a moment. And after a bit of reflection, he said, "I don't really care. I've already told you that I'm not a threat to them. I don't have a problem anymore. It's all their problem."

Peter studied the change in his hand. Then he said, "Look, things are heating up here. I was arrested the other day and the cops took some guns and other things from an apartment some of us rented a while back. I'm out on bail and there will be a hearing soon. You had best stay away from here. Like I said."

Standing outside on the deck of the ferry returning to the island, peering out at the choppy waves, he thought about what Peter had said. Was he really also a possible target for the FBI and the Red Squad? Could they also decide to pay him a visit out on the island? It all felt like such a dirty business. It had felt so much better to be part of the mass civil disobedience of the peaceniks. They were completely honest and open with everyone about everything they thought and did in opposition to militarism. Guns against guns was just seeming like such a self defeating proposition to him of late.

"Watching the waves always seems to set me free from my daily cares," spoke a young man Skeeter hadn't noticed until now, standing right next to him at the railing. He was of medium height, slim and light haired. They could have almost been brothers if not for his angelic smile that contrasted so sharply with Skeeter's grimly serious look.

"Sorry, I didn't see you there. Are you new to the island? I haven't seen you before," Skeeter said as he looked up from his fixation on the waves.

"Yes. I came here because of the Chinook Learning Center."

"Nice place," said Skeeter.

"I like a lot of what they're doing there. To be honest, I've been kind of adrift since I came home from my time overseas."

"Yeah, me too. Nam?"

"No. I was in the Peace Corps in Nepal for a couple years."

"Cool. Make peace, not war, brother." And he smiled and flashed him a peace sign.

"Well, here we are at the dock. See you." And they went their separate ways. But Skeeter felt a slight lift in his spirits. The light...

The weeks passed and he began to take more of an interest in things around him again. He replaced a rotted board on the little porch. He tuned the engine of the old truck and changed the oil. It got easier at times to forget the past as it receded in memory.

There came a day when he thought it might be alright if he and Austin never did find each other again in this life. And after that thought entered his mind something new and a bit strange started happening to him. Every once in a while he would be talking to someone, and he would hear something in his voice or a phrase or some such, and he would realize that he had unconsciously picked that up from her. There were even gestures, mannerisms that he'd never used before, that he seemed to have adopted. And when he thought about it, they really did remind him of her. She was no longer physically present in his life, but she hadn't totally disappeared either. There was something of her spirit that stayed with him. So was this what was meant by that hocus pocus, slippery stuff the holy liked to call someone's spirit? That part that didn't die or disappear when the physical body went away. It wasn't so mysterious after all. It did surprise him though, just how much she had infused him with some of her own spirit in the short while he had known her.

The spring time gave way to full summer. The trees and understory and ground cover of his forest world took on their full mantle of calming, lovely shades of green. The skunk cabbage bloomed in the marshes. Wild bees and wasps hummed contentedly in the forest understory. Bird song and wind song surrounded him during the day, and the gentle, enticing hoot of an owl occasionally floated to his ears at night.

He soon discovered the pleasure of spending an afternoon in quiet, solitary observation of life in a pond. He and his dog would venture out into the woods behind their cabin and find a good spot for just sitting at the edge of one of the little ponds that dotted the landscape.

In late spring and early summer there were tadpoles in various stages of metamorphosis, on their way to becoming frogs and toads, swimming around in the algae-encrusted water. And if he was observant he might see a frog half-hidden behind rocks or debris at the bottom of the pond.

Looking out across the pond, typically there might be a bed of cattails along the edge somewhere and maybe some pond lilies. And if he was observant, he might see a Bittern on its nest in the reeds, with its head tilted upward so that its long, slender brown neck and beak blended with the surrounding stalks of the cattails.

Other birds would come and go with the passage of time. Maybe a Red-winged Blackbird would perch in the reeds for a while or a swallow would swoop down over the pond in search of mosquitoes or flies. Other creatures also appeared in or near the ponds. Dragonflies, water bugs, garter snakes and frogs were a common sight.

One day he even came across an opossum lying dead as a doornail by the side of a pond. They were still rare on the island, but there were rumors of a few more here in recent years. He knew he was dead, because there were flies buzzing around the carcass, and he prodded him with a stick several times just to be sure. To this day though, he still wonders if he really was dead, or just "playing possum". He never saw that dead carcass again on future days, and there were always plenty of opossum tracks in the mud along the edges of that pond.

The meadows that occurred in larger clearings or bordered his woods were also worthy of many hours of observation. He kind of wished he had a camera so that he could take the same photo of the exact same frame of field over the course of the weeks from early April through August, because he was so impressed by the stunning cyclical changes that the fields would undergo during the growing season. From the first spring greens through the succession of blooms of various wildflowers, the field would change from pale green to darker shades of green and then a pale yellow brown as the grass died back. The field might be dotted with bright yellow and white heads of daisies at one time, with occasional bright splashes of the blue or creamy white of foxglove, and then the whole field would later take on a purple haze as the vetch came into bloom.

As summer passed the grass and the flowering plants turned into dry stalks full of seeds that fed insects, birds and mice. With an abundant food supply and cover for nesting, a great web of creatures made their homes there. Big strong Ring-necked pheasants, mostly escapees from the state pheasant farm on the outskirts of Coupeville, were among the most impressive of the birds, but there were also hawks, that circled the fields from high above in search of mice. The Killdeer were always entertaining, the way they would fake an injury, hopping along the ground with one wing dragging limply, while crying pitifully, in hopes that he would chase after them and away from the vicinity of some nest full of eggs hidden in plain view somewhere in the field.

There was the frantic flight of hundreds of grasshoppers, as he would make his way through the tall grass of summer. And when he would part the tall stems of grass and peer down at their base there were always ants, red army ants that would bite you if you weren't careful, friendlier black ants and tiny red ants. And as evening would come on in summer time there was always the song of frogs or toads.

The wood lots also had their residents. The small, feisty reddish brown Douglas squirrels lived in nests in the fir and hemlock trees and buried a portion of the fir cone crop away for their winter food supply. And, of course, what they didn't find that winter would sprout into little trees in the spring.

There were big, multi-hued green trees everywhere you looked. Big leaf maples, and an occasional native silver birch, and the typical mixed forests of alder, fir, hemlock, spruce and cedar.

By mid summer there were red and dark blue huckleberries to harvest in the shady woods, and by late summer there were also ripe Himalayan blackberries wherever the sun shone bright and no humans went to special effort to eradicate the vigorous, long wickedly thorned vines. He gorged himself on the ripe fruit in the season of ripe blackberries.

One day while out on a walk, he came across a man sitting in a wheel chair in a clearing in the woods. Skeeter gaped at the incongruity of it. "Hey, there," he called out to the man. "What brings you out here, to our woods?" He asked.

The fellow studied the ruddy, sun-burnished young man and his busy little dog for a moment. Then he said, "it was my van. A buddy dropped me off near here to enjoy a day in the woods. Your woods, you say? I didn't see any signs?"

"Just an expression. How about our woods, including you then?"

"That sounds good to me." And the man gave him a little grin.

"How long you out here for?" Skeeter asked.

"I got here at around sunrise. I'll probably stay til sunset."

"What do you do all that time?"

"Just sit and take it all in."

Skeeter considered that. Here was a guy so crippled that he could barely walk across a room. But, yet, here he was, out in a clearing in the woods, seated in a wheel chair. Not for a few minutes, like Skeeter, who was way too restless and energetic to stay put for long. No, he sat there for hours on end. "And what do you take in?" Skeeter asked.

"Oh, you'd be surprised at the amazing things that happen. Birds perch on my shoulder. Deer, rabbits and squirrels calmly go about their lives right in front of me. And I like to sketch some of them, and photograph them at times."

Skeeter thought about that. "Yeah, I get it. You do see amazing things." And he realized that this guy really did experience things a more "able-bodied" person would likely never find the patience to know. Here he had encountered a guy he had wanted to feel sorry for, but now he didn't.

And Skeeter found that he had thoughts in his solitude that he deemed worthy to commit to paper, in the event that he might someday have an opportunity to share them. One afternoon, sitting against a tree out at the edge of a fern bedecked clearing in the forest, he penned the following:

"When I get bored and lonely out here in these woods by myself, I usually try to do something to distract myself, read a book, listen to the radio or some music on a cassette tape.

But today I tried doing just the opposite when I found myself alone and beginning to feel that familiar fear of boredom or loneliness. Instead of reaching for the radio or a book, I sat down and thought about just how bored and lonely I was.

I let myself be bored and lonely and let myself have nothing to interest me or to do, and no need to seek anyone or anything out to end this situation.

Now that I had gotten this far I said to myself, in fact, there is really nothing I want to do but just sit here doing absolutely nothing.

And I told myself something like this: I am going to sit here and do and think nothing for as long as I feel like it. The world can muddle along just fine for a while without me, and I really don't care. It won't really matter if I never do anything again.

And then I begin to feel a sort of pleasure in solitude. It doesn't last, as my mind begins to drift in all sorts of directions. Flights of fantasy, or memories of events and experiences come to me. Some thoughts come to me of things that I haven't thought about in years, and then I am struck by the thought of something that I hadn't really considered doing before.

I think these thoughts might be part of the real benefit of solitude. If life becomes too busy, or narrowed by fears or worries, and when I am in serious danger of losing sight of who I am and what I really want in life, these thoughts can bring me back to my senses.

I recently read in a book, *Demian*, by the author Herman Hesse, just how hard it is to follow those 'true promptings which arise out of our innermost selves.' Thoughts and feelings of what we truly desire in life only come in moments of solitude.

It is very difficult for most of us not to get caught up in the life around us. So we rarely can discover the real person inside us . But what amazes me though, is that one of the simplest ways to renew interest and enthusiasm in life, is to simply retreat from life once in a while."

It was thoughts like these that made him realize that life alone in the woods wasn't all that bad. But he knew it would be better with the right companions, and then his thoughts would turn to his parents on their little farm, and to Austin, and he would think about the others back at their little farm. He had stopped by a few times to see his parents, but he was reluctant to go by the farmhouse where Ross and the others still lived, knowing that it would only remind him of his banishment.

One day, after a trip out, he came back to find a fresh bullet hole in the door. He just stood there feeling the splintered hole with his finger. Jack. Wasn't it strange? It seemed like just about everyone could get along without him, but not Jack. He seemed to need to seek him out occasionally to give him some reminder of his status as a worthless piece of shit. And if Skeeter wouldn't make himself available out there in public, Jack was more than willing to come to him at home for the reminder. It was just plain nuts.

That night Skeeter slept badly. He tossed and turned in bed for what seemed like hours, and it wasn't until early morning that he finally fell into a deep sleep. When he awoke the next morning he felt refreshed in ways that he hadn't in years. Something had changed, over night. He couldn't quite put his finger on it, but he knew that he was not the same person who had gone to sleep the night before.

He got up and put his clothes on and fed his dog. Then he made himself a big breakfast of bacon and eggs and coffee, and big slices of bread slathered with plenty of butter and homemade blackberry jam from his mother's pantry.

Then he put on his brown hunting jacket and a dark stocking cap. He then searched the cabin for a box of thirty caliber rifle cartridges and got out the old hunting rifle that he had spent the winter restoring. It was now once again a precision instrument for killing, and Skeeter had a crystal clear idea of how he would like to use it today.

It took him less than an hour to reach the spot where he had waited for Jack near his house earlier that year. This time he once again set himself in a position for optimal sighting in on his prey and waited. It was still only seven in the morning, but nature was alive and active all around him. Birds were singing, squirrels were busy cutting Douglas fir cones from the tops of the trees to drop to the ground with a small clatter, and the wind made a shushing sound as it sieved through the conifer needles and brought brittle red alder and big leaf maple leaves fluttering to the ground.

Skeeter, however, was far too focused on the task at hand to notice any of it. He sat, almost in a trance-like state for nearly an hour before Jack finally emerged from his house. He appeared to be in a good mood this morning. There was a slightly self-satisfied little smirk on his face. He yawned and stretched and looked about him as if he were "master of all he surveyed."

It astonished Skeeter just how easy it actually turned out to be in the end to erase this blight from the planet. Jack stood nearly stock still, his attention captured by something near his house. Skeeter's arm was rock steady as he braced himself against a tree and took careful aim. His finger slowly and carefully squeezed the trigger as he had been taught to do. The bullet traveled from the barrel of his rifle to lodge itself in Jack's brain in a near instant. The report of the rifle shot's explosion reached his ears at

about the same time as he saw Jack's body crumple to the ground in a
lifeless heap.

He returned to his truck and drove back down Amble Road to East
Harbor Road, took a left and continued on down to Goss Lake Road, where
he took another left. He followed it all the way down to the lake. He
parked at a rather secluded access to the lake and climbed down the hillside
to the heavily wooded shore. After carefully looking all around to make
sure that no one was watching, he hurled the rifle as far out into the lake as
possible, where it sunk into the depths. He then hurled the remaining shells
in after it. Then he quickly got back into the truck and drove home.

It amazed him how easy it all had actually turned out to be. No one
ever even came by to question him about Jack's murder. It seemed that he
had made so many enemies that the police didn't know where to begin
looking for likely suspects. And Skeeter traveled so far below their radar
these days that no one even thought of him when they began their
investigation.

It was an incredible weight lifted off Skeeter's shoulders, to be rid
of Jack once and for all. He could finally get on with his life, and he did.
He called Austin from the pay phone at Classic Road on the highway. He
was a little nervous, but when she answered, he just blurted it out. "Hi,
Austin. I sure have missed you."

"Same here, Skeeter. I've missed you terribly," she said. "And now
we're reconnected at last. I've waited for this..." It was so wonderful to hear
her voice again.

"Me too," he said. ""If only we had just talked to each other..."

"Well, that's all in the past now," she reassured him.

After they had talked a while and declared their undying love for
one another, he hung up, and got back in the truck and headed for home.
As he drove, he imagined how things would be. They would move in
together. Maybe get a nice little suburban ranch house on the cheap that
needed a little work, somewhere on the island.

And Skeeter, who would reintroduce himself to the community as
Robbie, would take a good, steady job, maybe hire in at the Boeing
Corporation's new aircraft assembly plant in Everett. Skeeter's life would
be blessed in so many ways that he had never imagined possible back in
the bad old days before he had murdered Jack.

When he awoke and found himself back in the cabin with Buddy, he wondered, 'how did I end up back here again?'

Fall came on and the trickle of alder leaves falling to the ground slowly began to turn into showers during windy periods, creating a sweet smelling carpet of yellow and brown on the forest floor. He brought buckets of Gravenstein apples home from his parents' orchard. And early in the morning before any neighbors were up, he would sneak down to Lagoon Point and catch a fish from the fall run of silver salmon by casting a lure out into the surf from shore.

As he stood by the shore of the Salish Sea, looking out toward the Strait of Juan de Fuca, that broad entrance to the great Pacific Ocean, he thought about how he much had taken this island home of his for granted in the past. It was all so familiar that he had rarely stopped to notice the smell of the salt water breeze, or to gaze into the clear, clean waters, the home of a myriad of wondrous sea creatures, from tiny krill to enormous gray whales, from subtle phosphorescent algae to expansive beds of bull kelp, or to just listen to the soothing rhythm of the surf as it endlessly churned and polished the particles of sand, gravel and stone of the seashore. Now he savored every moment that he joined in the food chain here, with his own rhythmic casting into the surf for a meal from the sea's bounty.

The neighbors on the beach were so grumpy, that he preferred to go down there as soon as it was light and be out before they got out of bed. He would have preferred the state park, but the steps down to the beach had washed out in a storm and the park system couldn't seem to find the money to replace them. It was a sad statement on public priorities. There was plenty of money for weapons no one but a madman would ever dare use, but barely a cent to allow hundreds of families the pleasure of a day at the beach at South Whidbey State Park.

As he sat there in his cabin frying a fish in a cast iron pan on the wood stove, and cooking up a pot of applesauce, he thought about the gang at the farm, and he thought about taking them a fish. And then he thought about the lines from a poem in a little volume that he had found by that great native son, Midwestern American poet Carl Sandburg:

"Fish to swim a pool in your garden

Flashing a speckled silver,
A basket of winesaps filling your room
With flame dark for your eyes
And the tang of valley orchards for your nose,
Such a beautiful pail of fish,
Such a beautiful peck of apples,
I cannot bring you now.
It is early and I am not yet footloose."

And he would remember why he rarely visited anyone. Until this thing with Jack was resolved, one way or another, it was best if he stayed away from them.

Chapter Fourteen

Another winter approached. The November sky was filled with dark, angry looking clouds that held serious bucketsful of rain. He sat inside the small cabin content to simply watch the cold rain, close to the hot wood stove, with Buddy settled on a warm blanket at his feet, with a warm mug of coffee in his hands.

It was during the long, dark nights of that November that he began to seriously examine his life for the first time. He continued to read books that his companions at the farm had suggested to him. More of Henry David Thoreu's *Walden Pond,* and he added Leo Tolstoy's *War and Peace* to his list. And another one that engaged his interest was Alan Watts *The Book- on the taboo against knowing who you are.* Where the religious philosophy of his childhood failed to sufficiently explain things, Alan Watts' interpretation of Eastern philosophy seemed to help:

"There was never a time when the world began, because it goes round and round like a circle, and there is no place on a circle where it begins. ... so, too, there is day and night, waking and sleeping, living and dying, summer and winter. You can't have any one of these without the other, because you wouldn't be able to know what black is unless you had seen it side-by-side with white, or white unless side-by-side with black."

These thoughts of Alan Watts stirred his mind as the rains clattered on the roof and the wind whispered in the dark and stirred the trees, and his fire became reduced to ash as midnight soon became one a.m. And there were other words as well that struck a new chord with him, such as the lines penned by H.D. Thoreau: *" To insure health, a man's relation to Nature must come very near to a personal one, he must be conscious of a friendliness in her; when human friends fail or die, she must stand in the gap to him."*

As he stood in the doorway of the cabin, looking out on the dawning of a new day, he wondered how he had failed for so long to really see the world around him? And why did so many pursuits seem so trivial to him now? And as he watched the alder leaves fade from green to yellow and brown he inevitably thought about the fundamental nature of life and death. He tried to imagine himself as an old man with someone like Austin in his life. Imagination, however, only seemed to serve him within certain limits. He couldn't imagine anything that far ahead. So, what to do? Carry on.

The days passed and a new calm settled over Skeeter. Even his dreams began to reflect this. One night he dreamed that he was back in combat. He was in the truck being transported to an outpost in the jungle. Suddenly, instead of a mortar barrage, the truck was attacked by a great mass of some sticky, gooey substance. They were all covered with the gooey mess. It was nearly impossible to clutch his rifle. Then the enemy came rushing out of the jungle, laughing at the whole truckload of them.

'What the hell?' thought Skeeter. He couldn't use his rifle to defend himself. None of them could. They were helpless. Stuck in the gooey mess. He knew then that they were about to be captured.

The enemy soldiers approached them, smiling. ""Taste it!" shouted one of them.

'What?' thought Skeeter. But he tasted the sticky mess that covered him. Karo corn syrup! No wonder they were all such an incapacitated mess.

"This is the new face of future war," laughed one of the enemy soldiers. "We will now disarm you, hose you down good, and then see about shipping you back to your homeland, and hope you don't do anymore mischief here in our country."

Skeeter woke with a smile on his face. What a silly dream!

It was about one in the morning not long after that Skeeter and Buddy were startled out of a sound sleep by a rifle shot quite close to the cabin, followed by the shattering of glass as the window by the door shattered into a hundred pieces. This was soon followed by the distant sound of a truck engine starting up and then receding into the distance. 'This has got to end, finally, somehow,' thought Skeeter as he began cleaning up the shards of glass scattered around the cabin floor.

Later that morning Skeeter heard another truck engine. His first reaction was to scan the cabin in search of his shotgun. In recent times he had grown lax about security. A while back he had wrapped all of his weapons up in an old wool army blanket and stuffed them back in some deep cubby hole at the back of the little loft above his bed.

Now he wondered if that had been all that wise a decision. As the truck drew nearer he could tell that it was a small truck. Definitely not Jack. And he relaxed a bit.

When the truck finally pulled up next to his own, he could see that it was a small, white truck with a county logo on the side. Two men got out. One was an older man with wire rimmed glasses, who carried a clip board with some papers attached. The other was younger, maybe in his thirties, who wore a green baseball cap. He had a cardboard square in his hands.

They approached the door and Skeeter opened it before one of them could knock on it. They looked uneasy, like this wasn't their favorite duty. "What's up, man?" Skeeter asked.

The younger of the two said, "We got a complaint. A call. Someone reporting that you had an illegal cabin out here in the woods."

"Really? Illegal? Is that right? Who would of thought..." He answered.

" Our county adopted the Uniform Building Code last year. You can't just go building cabins out in the woods without a permit. Didn't you know that?"

"Heck, no. Here I am way the hell out in the woods. The nearest house nearly a mile away. No power lines. Not even much of a road to the door. I didn't think anybody would give a damn."

"Well, somebody did. He reported you this morning."

"So I'm going to staple this Stop Work order next to the door and take a picture of the place."

"Well, go ahead. I don't plan on doing anything more on it anyway."

The man frowned at that. "You need to come down to the Building Department and find out what you have to do to get legal."

"Sure, man." He answered, with no intention of doing anything of the kind.

"Now I need to measure the dimensions of your cabin in order to add the building to your assessment," said the older man, while staring down at his clipboard. He was obviously uncomfortable with this whole thing. He probably knew that there were all sorts of old cabins in their rural county that were unrecorded. Nobody cared except the occasional neighbor who wanted to make someone else's life a little more miserable. They never got calls like this from someone just doing their civic duty or concerned about the health and welfare of a neighbor in a substandard dwelling. It was always just a grudge of some sort.

"Hey, man, what about this proposed law, this owner builder amendment to the building code. Could I apply for that?"

The younger man frowned. It will be up for a vote soon. But every county official, the sheriff's department, fire chief, you name it, is opposed to it."

'Yeah,' thought Skeeter. 'Too much freedom for the guys in charge. And he forgot to mention all the people who make their money off a helpless population of consumers, who can't fix a car or put up a shed, let alone a cabin to live in.' But he said, "Glad we get to vote on it."

"Well, it won't do you any good right now. You're in violation of the law. You're not supposed to be living in this place, unless it is permitted by the county. The building has to be approved and, of course, you need to have an approved septic and water system, and a road that fire trucks and rescue vehicles can drive down."

Skeeter felt like there was a noose tightening around his neck. All he had wanted when he started paying the $75 a month with no down payment for this piece of the big forest was a place to escape civilization. But then, he was the one who had brought this down on his head by pissing off Jack the way he had. "Oh, you forgot to mention the cops. They need to be able to drive in so that they can arrest my ass when they don't like what I'm doing."

The man gave Skeeter a flinty glare at that, and said, "yeah, and that."

"I guess the dog and I will have to sleep out in the truck from now on to satisfy the law."

At this the fellow stared at him for a moment, then said, "It would probably still be illegal, unless you park out on the county access road." At this the fellow with him looked at his coworker as if he were an idiot to suggest such a thing.

Skeeter caught that look and understood the meaning. Sometimes the law really was an ass, and those who insisted on enforcing the letter of it. Then the two of them abruptly turned and headed back toward their truck. Skeeter watched them, and then he shouted to their backs, "you two gentlemen have a nice day now."

The younger man turned his head and shot him a quick, dirty look, while the older man just hunched his shoulders a bit and looked as if he wanted to be out of there as quickly as possible. Then the older fellow muttered, just loud enough for Skeeter to hear, "Just doing our job."

'Yeah,' thought Skeeter. 'So were the guards at Dachau.' Then he said to himself, 'got to lighten up, hell, they aren't the Gestapo. The times they are a changing. That's all. Doesn't mean I have to like it, no more than the Indians who used to live here and got pushed off their land by the white man's laws. But you have to resist. Good thing there are some folks who are trying to amend the law to make it easier for poor folks to make a home for themselves here. Maybe I had better get off my butt and go out and help them in their campaign.'

That night Skeeter was startled out of a deep sleep by a tremendous shaking of the earth under his small cabin. As he became more aware of the tremors, he rolled himself out of bed and onto the floor next to the bed. Buddy whined and huddled close to him on the floor. The cabin pitched and rolled from side to side, as if he were riding a roller coaster, and there was a sound as if a freight train were rumbling past his cabin door. Things crashed all around him and he could hear the sound of shattering glass as the windows gave way. After about four minutes the tremors stopped, and after a few more minutes, he and Buddy emerged from the rubble. He dressed and crawled out of the ruined cabin.

He stepped outside and studied the wreckage. The cabin had been tossed off its cedar post foundation, and one wall had partially collapsed, bringing part of the roof down as well. As he looked about, he could see big branches and whole trees strewn about the forest floor. Just getting out to the road in his car might take half a day of chainsaw work.

After some ten more minutes had passed, he heard the sound of people screaming off in the distance, in the direction of Lagoon Point, three quarters of a mile to the west. Then there was a tremendous roar as the ocean surged onto the lowland beach area of the lagoon and crashed against the high clay bluff. Then it was suddenly eerily silent.

It was then that he awoke from the terrible nightmare. As his mind cleared and he thought about all that he had dreamed, he muttered to himself, "Thank God that we don't live in a region where such terrible earthquakes can occur. The poor people of Alaska and California always have to live under that threat. Lucky for us, it can't happen here.

That next morning Skeeter prepared for a hunting trip. He dressed in dark green pants and jacket. He cleaned the pistol, and he finally completed the reassembly of the old Japanese rifle that had been in need of repair ever since it had arrived in the US in his dad's old duffel bag. Then he wrote a note that he left on the table:
"Dear folks(and friends),
If you are reading this, I didn't succeed at the hunt I went on. It was a risky plan in any event. But not to worry. All in all, life lately has been okay. After a few crummy years after returning from the service, I seem to have made some progress in getting my life together. I think that the biggest lesson I take from this year is that it isn't about me. I'm not the center of the universe, but I'm not alone. In fact, without you and this beautiful world that surrounds me, I would not exist. You, we, together all make it happen. And if I wasted some time wallowing in self-pity, bitterness and anger, I don't do that anymore. I wish you all well. Wish I could repay all of the kindness you've shown me. Life is good. Sorry I couldn't stick around to enjoy more of it with you. Sorry to go missing like this.
Skeeter, Robbie Jenson"

Then he collected a small knapsack of gear, tucked the pistol in his belt, and stowed the old Japanese rifle behind the seat of the truck. He set the dog, now more often called Buddy, with his bowl with water and food outside. He picked him up in his arms and gave him a bit of a tummy rub and let him lick his face. Then he set him down and tried to make him understand that he was to stay. But when he got in the truck to drive off, there in the rear view mirror he could see the dog running after him down the road. And so he returned to the cabin and tried it again with the same result. It was only on the third try that he finally succeeded in getting the dog to reluctantly stay as he drove off.

Skeeter drove the old truck slowly and carefully out to the paved road. It was still rather beat up looking, but he had long ago replaced the muffler and done a brake job and tuned the engine up.

When he finally reached the corner of East Harbor and Brainer Roads, he looked for the place he had hidden the truck before. He finally found the almost hidden lane. He followed it back in about fifty yards and was about to park when he spotted a little cabin on a rise just ahead. 'I never saw that before,' he thought to himself.

He thought that he had better check it out before he parked here. He shut down the engine of the truck and got out and studied the little cabin. He could hear faint music coming from inside. Unusual music, it sounded like a chorus of men's voices were harmonizing in ways that he had never heard before.

As he stood there listening, the door opened. A slim, blond haired young man, holding a paintbrush, peered out. When he saw Skeeter, he gave a small wave of greeting.

"Hi," said Skeeter. "I never noticed a cabin back here. Last time I parked my truck here it was dark, and I didn't see anything. Sorry to bother you."

"If you want to park here for a walk in the woods, I don't mind. But you look like you are out hunting. Not so sure I want you doing that here," the fellow answered in what sounded like maybe a Scandinavian or German accent to Skeeter.

"Oh, don't worry. I'm not planning to shoot any game."

"Good. You look a little familiar. Do I know you?"

Skeeter approached the door. "We might have met before. I'm not sure." And he could see canvases, paint supplies and brushes set out on a long table along the back wall of the small cabin, next to an easel that held his most recent painting. "So you're an artist?" He said.

"Yes, friend let me use this cabin. It's a great place to paint."

"Where you from?"

"Holland," he replied. "And you?"

"From here," Skeeter said. 'This island is getting more interesting all the time,' he thought. 'Now we've got Dutch artists living out in the woods.' And from what he could see, the guy really knew how to paint. The painting on his easel was of a beautiful scene from nature, but there was some dream-like quality to the work, and it also had some other unusual feel about it that he couldn't quite place. Then he realized that the work reminded him somehow of the writings of Alan Watts on Eastern philosophy that he had been reading. There was the spirit that Watts had tried to convey in words, in this work. 'The picture worth a thousand words,' he thought.

"Well, I'd better not bother you anymore. Nice picture. I like the music on your cassette player too. It all reminds me of someone I've been reading lately. You ever hear of Alan Watts?"

"Of course, and you're perceptive about the painting," he answered. "Come by again and we'll talk some time."

"I'd like that," Skeeter answered as he retreated toward the truck and the artist closed the cabin door and returned to his work.

'Make art, not war,' he thought as he pulled the gear he would need out of the truck. When he pulled the rifle out, the artist stepped back out of his cabin and shouted, "hey, I thought you said you weren't going to hunt."

"I promise, I won't shoot any animals. Really," he replied.

"Okay, but I don't see what you need the gun for. Can't you just walk the woods without it?"

He paused, a little taken aback by this. "I suppose I could, and probably should..." His voice trailed off as he started off into the woods, leaving the artist looking a bit puzzled, watching him go from the porch of his cabin.

It was mid afternoon by the time he finally managed to position himself within visual range of the house. He was expecting Jack to return from the bar in another hour or two. His idea was to catch him in his sites unaware, and then announce a few facts of life to Jack.

Some favored simply aiming for the biggest part, go for the middle, to assure that you didn't miss. That might not bring him down though. And we all know what they say about how dangerous a wounded beast can be. A little low and you have a gut shot. Terribly messy, but plenty painful. Skeeter thought that he might go for that.

But then he thought better of that. He would rather try for a head shot. It would make for a better chance of bringing him down, first shot. If it were an accurate shot. So many ifs involved in this ugly business.

He thought he wouldn't mind it if he could manage somehow to get him restrained in duct tape. In that condition maybe Skeeter could talk some sense into him. Right. That made a lot of sense. Getting him restrained would be nearly impossible. A nice clean ambush made the most sense. The rifle propped securely on some stationary post, a tree or log or rock or something. Then, just slowly squeeze the trigger and put an end to all this craziness.

The wait was agonizing. He didn't want to have to think this through anymore. There was no simple answer. But prison for ridding the world of such a piece of vermin. How could he accept that?

After about an hour a truck pulled up in front of the house and Jack got out. The time for thought, for reflection, for dithering, was over. Skeeter stood up from his hiding place and braced himself on a nearby tree and then leveled the rifle on him. His shoulders trembled. No, he said. Don't you get scared. Not for this. Get more serious than you have ever been before in your life. And then he felt himself regain focus and a strange kind of calm came over him. His heartbeat normalized, and he knew he was ready. He drew a bead on Jack's head.

Then he said to himself, 'No, Jack needs to know what's happening to him, what he's brought down on himself.' So Skeeter walked out to where Jack could see him. Then he raised the rifle once again and aimed it at the biggest part of him. Jack just stared at him, a bit dazed and startled at first, kind of like a deer caught in the headlights. Then a slightly cruel, almost self-satisfied smile appeared on his face. And he said, "You just better hope you don't miss, because I will be all over you then, and I promise you that you will not like it one bit."

"You always have liked a good fight, haven't you, Jack," Skeeter heard himself reply. "You are just one mean son of a bitch."

"That's me, alright. But just know that even though there is no way you could ever get the best of me in a fair fight, I ain't the least bit scared of some cowardly attack by a worthless little prick like you. Go ahead and pull the trigger, you chicken shit runt."

Skeeter got deadly still at this. He took a breath, and when he knew the real moment of truth had arrived, he calmly lowered the rifle and looked Jack in the eye, and in the calmest voice he'd ever known, he said, "Time to settle this once and for all, Jack. I am sick of running from you or feeding my fantasies of gunning you down and being rid of you. So it comes down to this..."

And he threw the rifle down at Jack's feet, and then he pulled the pistol out of his belt and tossed that down as well. Then he turned and started walking away.

Jack stared momentarily at the weapons at his feet, and then he reacted, quickly gathering up the pistol and rushing after Skeeter. When he caught up with him, he shouted: "It's not over until I say it's over.'" And he pointed the pistol at Skeeter's back.

"Okay, it's for you to decide when it's over, but I'm through," Skeeter said, with a slight tremor entering his voice now.

"Turn around and look at me, you little prick," Jack growled, all the while holding the pistol fixed on Skeeter's back.

Skeeter turned around to face Jack. He tried to remain calm, but his heart was pumping like mad, and he could feel a throbbing in his temple, and he started to feel a bit woozy, as if, maybe, all of this were happening in a dream.

"Good, now take your medicine," Jack said as he fired a shot that kicked up dust mere inches from Skeeter's toes.

Skeeter involuntarily flinched and a shudder ran through his body. He feared that he might piss his pants too. But then he regained control of himself. It was alright. This was exactly what he had chosen in the end. No more running, no more hiding, no more cringing either.

Then Jack fired a second round. This one caught Skeeter squarely in the big toe.

At first he just gaped in disbelief, then the blood began to ooze out of the hole in his shoe and the pain started. It was sharp, almost unbearable, and he tried not to scream out. He slumped forward slightly and tottered a bit in place, with a tight grimace on his face.

"Maybe that one didn't make enough of an impression on you, so try this one," and he fired again. This time winging Skeeter in the other ankle.

Skeeter fell to the ground and began to groan in pain. Jack just spit on the ground in front of him, and said, with a nasty little grin on his face, "Don't you ever fuck with me, ever again." Then he walked back toward his house with the pistol and collected the rifle and went in the door.

Skeeter lay on the ground momentarily, and then started crawling toward the edge of the yard, in the direction where he had left his truck. It was incredibly painful. His ankle bone had been damaged, and although there wasn't a whole lot of blood there, his big toe was a bloody mess, and all of it hurt like hell. All the same, he slowly lifted himself to his feet, and he made progress, limping along, although every movement was sheer agony. Eventually he crawled into the truck and after a brief rest, and using every ounce of his willpower to resist the dizziness that threatened to overwhelm him, he finally got the truck started and rolling toward Whidbey General Hospital

Epilogue

Let there be peace. And let it begin with me.

Some forty years have passed since the day he confronted Jack out front of his house. So much has happened since then. Skeeter has changed, and the island has changed in so many ways. As he walks down Anthes Street in Langley Skeeter looks about him in wonder, and he muses: 'I suppose my life could be very different today if a few things had gone differently, but I suppose you could say that about the whole island, and the whole world, if you wanted to.'

He is still rather amazed by the fact that he mended so well after Jack maimed him with his gun so long ago. He still sometimes just marvels at the wonder of it all. If it didn't change Jack all that much that day, Skeeter knows that he was transformed.

Today, as he occasionally is wont to do, he meets Jack on the street here in Langley. Jack has been living quietly for some years now, after serving his last sentence for assault. He had worried that Skeeter would press charges against him. He had even come by once to see if he needed to lean on him to keep quiet. Skeeter had simply told him: "We're through. Now just go home and get on with your life. That's what I intend to do."

When he sees Jack now, he tries to convey, in a friendly nod, that he really doesn't harbor any ill will toward him. Jack just ignores him, but Skeeter can't help but wonder sometimes if maybe he too learned a few things over the years. Skeeter only knows that he has ridded himself of the hatred and fear that once ruled his own life.

As Jack passes on down the sidewalk in the opposite direction, Skeeter mutters to himself, "tend to your own garden..."

He passes the Good Cheer Thrift Store and walks on down to the corner of First Street. He glances off in the direction of the exotic rug shop, "Music for the Eyes" and then rounds the corner in the direction of the theatre. The chance encounter with Jack just now has stirred his mind a bit. 'What was Jack, really?' He asks himself. 'Not the personification of evil. More like a terribly sad human being.'

He stares about him in wonder at his little town of Langley, all spiffed up and ready for a whole new season of tourists. It's still a friendly little town. The modest downtown has retained the charming little hundred year old storefronts that were not so new even in his youth. The Clyde Theatre is still here, but the Doghouse Tavern just sits there vacant now, for several years, looking ever the more decrepit, but perhaps not beyond repair.

There are those who say that you really can't call it much of a town anymore. They sort of think of it as more of "a charming little boutiqueville by the sea". But he still likes to come by, even if you can no longer get gasoline, hardware or lumber here. Store space is at a premium to cater to the growing tourist trade. But he still enjoys the fact that you can meet your fellow humans eye to eye here as you walk the streets, instead of greeting them through window glass as one does elsewhere, where drive around shopping is the norm, in the sprawl of the business districts of bigger towns.

He has so many memories of so many people, come and gone. Fine people and wretched souls in need of redemption. Like everywhere. He has his ghosts who follow him everywhere he goes these days. Not exactly haunting him as filling his mind and spirit with enduring memories. As he walks down the sidewalk on First Street he thinks back. 'How I miss some of my old friends. Especially when I think about what we did together.' And the enduring physical world reminds him of other times. Here is the old Doghouse, for example, where he first saw Austin one evening.

'The old Cold War is heating up and maybe the missiles are back on high alert. And then there is this new threat of global climate change. Who knows where that will lead...' He muses. 'But it isn't all bad. People still do clever things, and Langley is still pleasant to visit. Lord knows we could use more places that are this quiet and peaceful to just sit in company with friends.'

A smile lights up his face as he remembers a silly dream he had the night before. In the dream all of the owners of storage units full of tables, beds, chairs, toasters, silverware, and the like, suddenly declared that it would all now be available to the homeless. Thousands of desperately poor, homeless people, all over the country, suddenly had warm, dry places to sleep, with all sorts of comforts, from plush sofas to warm, clean beds. And all of the people who had been hoarding all of this junk, that they had no real use for, were relieved of the further burden.

'What a silly dream,' he thinks to himself. 'But then, nearly anything that can be dreamed, is made a bit more possible.'

'There was a day when you could build a little cabin and live in it without government intrusion. Not so easy anymore. But then again, there have been other things come along since the good old days that I don't mind at all. I sure appreciate some modern things around here, such as the free buses that roam the island daily, picking people up and dropping them off from the far south end of the island all the way up to Deception Pass in the north. With my gimpy, arthritic limbs I do appreciate the way they've made it easier for me to get some places without a long hike.'

Just last week he took the bus and train all the way into Seattle. After a brief visit to the old bookstore down in the Pike Place Market, run nowadays by a whole new crop of idealistic young people, he headed down to the wharf. It was SeaFair time and there was a big crowd gathered to watch the navy ships in the harbor. As friends circled the ships in kayaks and sailboats decked out with banners urging cuts in military spending, he unfurled his own banner that read "Veterans for Peace," and he began handing out leaflets to the crowd gathered to watch the navy ships, explaining their concerns about excessive and unnecessary military spending.

His walk takes him down a little passageway between buildings onto Second, where he spies a bench outside The Commons Coffeehouse and sits down. Then he sees a friend and she joins him. "I love the one I heard the other day," he tells her. "Someone asks, what would you tell someone from the 1970's about the big changes in life since their time? And the answer was: in our time everybody carries around a little hand held device that allows us to access most of the accumulated knowledge of the entire human race almost instantaneously. However, most of us use it to share cat pictures and have petty arguments with relatives."

"And have you been back to volunteer at Enso House since the passing of your dear one?" She asks.

After a brief shadow passes over his face, Skeeter says, "No, I plan to go over to the Good Cheer Food Bank to help out this morning."

Skeeter looks around him at the coffeehouse. He sees a new crop of young people have arrived on the island this spring. They just continue to come from all over and they seem to enjoy what they find here, not unlike Austin and Ross and the gang back when. He loves to see their energy and passion and idealism. And they are so fresh and look so cute, like puppies at times, in their gamboling gait and dance.

He carries a cup of coffee over from the counter and sits down again at the table with his old friend. He opens his iPad and calls up a webpage on the Internet. "You have got to hear this," he says. "The young folks who come here may not know all of the dimensions of what they are seeing around them. But they do see it all with fresh eyes. It is all so beautiful as seen through their eyes. Let me read you what one of them wrote the other day, posted on her Facebook page: *"Farming here at the Greenbank Farm school is not your typical 9-5 job – there are many tasks that are best done at night or sunrise; for example, irrigating is best done from nightfall to sunrise when the winds are calm... When I head out to the field at 10pm to switch irrigation valves, I know there's a big pair of eyes watching as I move through the red clover – a Great Horned Owl has taken up residence at the farm this year, perching on our trellis lines and hunting for voles every night. We couldn't ask for a better night watchman! And he isn't shy, either – we sat twenty feet away from each other one night. ...I know so many of you already love and appreciate the beautiful perch atop the ridge, the walking trails, and the farm fields during daylight that I felt compelled to share a slice of the night scene here. Come enjoy the sunset sometime! You might find some star-struck farmers spinning in circles, eyes to the skies..."*

He sets down the iPad. "I can understand if they don't want to sit still and hear stories about what went on here before they got here," he tells his friend. "They want to live in the present, to be present here. You can't really do that if you are dwelling on the past so much, like me."

And he can't help himself, as his mind drifts again to memories of "the old days" when the island was far more rural than it is today. When the towns were smaller, housing projects rare, and the beach communities consisted of small clusters of summer cottages and cabins, nothing like the big, boxy homes that often press against each other on postage stamp sized lots on so many beaches today.

Still, he is pleasantly surprised at the continued predominance of forest and farmland on the island. In the many years that he has watched this island's life, he is pleased to note that there is a growing love and respect for the land. More residents than ever before will make sacrifices to preserve the rural character of the island. They are willing to pay tax money that is then used to purchase wild lands that might otherwise be lost to development.

The European settlers of Whidbey Island took their rural environment for granted, because that described most of the continent before the mid twentieth century. Growing food, harvesting timber, harvesting wild food sources such as deer and salmon, this is just what most American families did back then. There had been conservation movements early in the century to establish the national park and forest systems and eventually further efforts were made to encourage conservation practices that would prevent things like the Great Dustbowl of the 1930's. However, it was not until the late nineteen sixties that many people started to get alarmed at the rapid pace of developments that were degrading the environment.

Few people would ever suggest today that it would be a good thing if Whidbey Island were mostly paved over and almost exclusively populated by human beings, their pets and machinery. It is also so heartening to see how many people who live here shop at the island's several thriving farmers markets, buying produce grown by a new crop of young farmers, and buying products of artisans carrying on many of the traditional crafts of the island's rural past. Who would have guessed that the steamroller of urbanization of most of the Puget Sound basin would stall on the islands of the Salish Sea, that new name for the large body of water of the bio-region.

As a steady stream of young people come and go from the coffeehouse bookstore, he studies them, and when he sees someone he thinks might benefit from some advice he has for them, he approaches their table. "Are you thinking at all maybe about a military career? You know, the new all volunteer army? And if he gets an affirmative answer he hands them a brochure prepared by The War Resisters League, and he urges them to read this before they make any decision.

When he is once more by himself on a park bench looking out on
Saratoga Passage, he pulls out a notebook that he found the other day
among his things. He begins reading the first poem in Austin's notebook:

*Sunday Service at South Whidbey State Park with the Quakers on Earth
Day*

Let each man and woman leave their
daily chores and cares
to walk barefoot along sandy, tranquil shores,
on a Sunday morning.

The humble and the mighty,
the well-to-do, those without shoes,
walking, laughing, singing
alone, or by twos and threes or fours,
under the glorious sky,
touched by wind, rain,
the sun.

Then and there, surrounded by
air, sand and water,
power and possession put behind,
forgotten for a moment,
in grace, all together,
no longer leaden, bound
or burdened,
we could soar
on newly sprouted wings!

When will life on earth
be recognized to be sufficient,
all we ever need or want
of heaven, of hell,
and the choice, there
for you, for me,

for everyone, now?

And then he comes upon a poem that brings it all back to him:

In the Classic U Forest, Autumn 1979

We were married beneath a tree named perseverance,
named majesty.
The Apache benediction of marriage was invoked
by our own appointed minister and a president in charge of saving trees,
beneath an ancient matriarch of trees.

"Now you will feel no cold.
For each will be warmth for the other.
Now you will feel no rain.
For each shall be shelter to the other.
Now there will be no more loneliness for you.
For one life lies before you.
Go now unto your dwelling place to begin
the time of your togetherness.
And may your days be long and good upon the earth."

The roof of our wedding cathedral
was as tall as the sky that day,
and music was provided by a choir
of mingled bird voices
hidden in the boughs and branches
round about.

We and a few close friends met by
the oldest single living creature
on this island,
a cedar tree
wider than our outstretched arms
and ever so tall and hundreds of years old.

What bride and groom were ever married
in greater splendor
than we within such a grove of trees?
In this case, a grove only recently
rescued from the merchant's chopping block
in a triumph of the human heart over indifference and greed.
May our marriage draw beauty,
strength and wisdom
from the scene of its inception.

They did not find each other again in this world until Austin eventually came back to the island for a visit about three months after Skeeter made that final visit to Jack's. By then, he was pretty much on the mend, and he was a frequent visitor over at the Nature Kids' farm.

That particular day he and Buddy dropped by to return some books that Skeeter had borrowed from the farm library. It was late afternoon and the sun was already setting in this northern latitude, it being just a few weeks after the winter solstice.

He could smell fresh bread just out of the oven as he stepped through the door, unannounced, with Buddy just a step behind. It was a sign of his relation to the farm that he didn't even bother to knock upon his arrival, but just let himself in as if he lived there.

There was someone sitting by the stove, wrapped in a light blanket, reading a book, but Skeeter didn't pay them any special mind at first. He was too busy holding the door open for the dog while making sure the pile of books in his arms didn't slip out of his grasp. Then when he saw Buddy beeline it to the figure in the chair, Skeeter's eyes followed him, and he saw her.

"Hey," he said.

"Hey to you too," she replied, as she looked up from her book, while reaching down to scratch behind the dog's ears.

"How's it going?" He asked.

"Okay," she answered. "How about you?"

"Oh, I can't complain. Kind of been hard to keep the cabin warm with this cold snap."

"It's been cold like this for a while, huh?"

"Yeah," he answered.

About then several other members of the household appeared from the kitchen carrying a tray with slices of Annie's freshly baked bread, slathered with butter and homemade blackberry jam.

"Hey there Skeeter. Look what we've got. Go get a mug and pour yourself some of the tea from the pot on the stove and come join us for some of Annie's bread," said Ross as he set the tray down on a small table near the stove.

Skeeter went in and got himself a mug of tea, still glancing over in Austin's direction, kind of studying her a bit, surreptitiously, trying to notice any changes in her appearance. From what he could tell, her hair was about the same, but unlike all of the pasty northerners in the room, she had a bit of color to her face from the southern sun, even in this winter season.

She was as comfortable with the crowd in this room as if she had never left. They laughed and joked and munched their buttered bread. There was music playing in the background. Something Irish with fiddles.

"Hey, you guys remember that toast and tea Skeeter fed us that first time we were all at his cabin?" Skeeter was a little embarrassed to have Ross bring that up.

"Yeah," said Annie, laughing. "Wonderbread! Remember? And to tell you the truth, I never enjoyed a piece of crappy, store bought American white bread so much in all my life as I did that night."

"Yeah, we were all starving by then, and it was like, midnight," laughed Austin.

He was afraid that someone would mention the fact that he had slammed the door in their faces when they first arrived at his cabin, but no one brought that up. And he just grinned, and said, "Okay, so my bread wasn't quite up to the high standards you were used to with Annie baking for you back here."

They invited him to stay for some of the soup they had prepared for supper, which he gratefully accepted. When it eventually came time for him and Buddy to head for home, Austin surprised him by saying, I'd like to come by some time and visit you."

"Sure," he said, sort of pleased, and also kind of trying not to make too much of it.

"How about Friday I come by and pick you up," he said. 'Was this a date he had just invited her on, to his place?' He wondered.

"Okay," she answered.

They "courted," from what Skeeter could recall, for almost a week. Getting together for a meal, or a walk, or just hanging around with the gang at the farm of an evening. Until finally they ran out of things to talk about one cold winter evening, sitting together by the stove at the farm. And touch replaced words, and then they retreated to Skeeter's old "shedroom" as they had called it. The others made an effort not to smile too obviously, and no one said a word, as they slipped out of the house together on their way to the small cabin, through a pitch black night filled with a million sparkling stars.

Note

The actual round up of orca whales in Penn Cove occurred in 1970. The
murder in front of The Doghouse in Langley occurred in the early 1980's.
The murder of the young woman in Greenbank occurred in 1977. The
protest of logging across from South Whidbey State Park took place
August 10, 1977. Professor Richard White's book *Land Use, Environment
and Social Change* was published in 1979. The shootout with white
supremacists in Greenbank actually took place around 1981. The owner
builder amendment to the county building code did pass in a public
referendum in the early 1980's. It was revoked by the county
commissioners in the late 1980's. The public protest at the Trident
submarine base on Hood Canal also took place as stated in the novel, on
May 22, 1977 with 300 arrests and 4,000 in attendance. Jack Miller was
the IWW participant in the Everett Massacre who was a frequent visitor to
the Left Bank Bookstore in the Pike Place Market in the 1970's. Members
of the George Jackson Brigade were arrested in 1976 and members of the
Left Bank Collective served time in jail that same year for noncooperation
with a grand jury convened to investigate left wing terrorist activity.
Cascade Community Center staff were also arrested in 1977 at protests of
the removal of tenants from low-income housing. The closure of the beach
at South Whidbey State Park due to washout of the stairway occurred
much later than 1977, but it lasted over two years and the stairway was
only repaired when a group of local volunteer carpenters rebuilt it with
lumber donated by local lumberyards. The ferry Kulshan transported
twenty cars at a time to and from Whidbey Island in 1977. Complaints
about navy jet noise and private takeover of public beach accesses on
Whidbey Island has been ongoing since the 1970's.

        The group, Save Whidbey Island For Tomorrow formed on central
Whidbey in 1976 to advocate for preservation of the rural environment.
Members of that group were instrumental in the creation of the Ebey's
Landing National Historic Reserve. Some of them joined allies from South
Whidbey from the group Save the Trees in the civil disobedience at South
Whidbey State Park in the summer of 1977. That effort eventually led to

preservation of the half mile of old growth forest there. It is now part of South Whidbey State Park.

The activists of the 1970's inspired further efforts to preserve the rural environment here in the 1980's and beyond. Many people today support the preservation work of the Whidbey Camano Land Trust. Others promote environmental education and stewardship through the organic farming and gardening organization South Whidbey Tilth, or work to preserve wildlife habitat here through the Whidbey Audubon Society. Today the Whidbey Institute continues the efforts to raise awareness of connections of nature and spirit at the former Chinook Learning Center.

The Orca Network today works to raise awareness of the whales of the Salish Sea and of the importance of providing them healthy and safe habitats. They will certainly see that no one ever again rounds up orca whales here for sale to aquatic amusement parks.

Many residents have also joined the Whidbey Environmental Action Network, a group that has helped prevent the conversion of many acres of forest and farmland to other uses here. That group began by organizing protests when a roving, multinational corporation purchased and logged thousands of acres here in one year's time in the 1980's. Many of those logs were shipped overseas, and much of the land was put up for sale for housing tracts. Recently 650 acres of that land was purchased and reclaimed as public forest wild land by the Whidbey Camano Land Trust.

Another large corporation bought the landmark Greenbank Loganberry Farm and concluded that the "highest and best use" for the farm would be to convert it to a housing project. They eventually chose to sell the farm to a mobilized public, and it is now Whidbey Island's first and only public-owned farm park. Unfortunately, however, they left the public a farm with depleted soil and polluted groundwater, the barn roofs rotting and the machinery gone to ruin. Much work has already been done and much more will be required to fully restore the landmark farm. Only an active, involved community has prevented these roving, multinational corporations from leaving such places irreparably damaged and degraded.

There is also a recently formed group on Whidbey Island that is challenging expanded military activity on the island and beyond. They are raising the alarm concerning operations that harm the public good, whether it be harm to wildlife, the environment or the human inhabitants of the region.

And today we know that we really should prepare for a big, potentially very devastating earthquake. It is not a matter of if it will occur, but the fact that it very possibly will occur within the lifetime of many of us living here today. Best to be prepared.